ATTACK OF THE RAITHS!

"Did you think I was going to let you have all the fun?" a soft voice whispered as Tahiri joined Anakin. She held her spear before her. "Let them attack first," Tahiri said quietly. "If they're anything like the womp rats on Tatooine, you'll be able to sense which way they'll strike a split second before they do—"

Tahiri's explanation was cut short as one of the raiths emitted a high-pierced whine and launched itself. She ducked sideways, keeping her spear vertical. The raith impaled itself on the sharp tip. Tahiri hardly noticed the thick green blood that sprang from the wound. She wrenched her spear out of the dead creature and turned to face the second rodent.

"Anakin, watch out!" Tahiri cried.

Anakin lunged sideways as a third raith flew toward him . . .

THIS BOOK
ALSO CONTAINS A PREVIEW OF
THE JUNIOR JEDI KNIGHTS'
NEXT EXCITING ADVENTURE:
PROMISES

The *Star Wars: Junior Jedi Knights* Series

STAR WARS.
Junior Jedi Knights
Lyric's World

Nancy Richardson

BERKLEY JAM BOOKS, NEW YORK

Based on a story outline by Kevin J. Anderson
and Rebecca Moesta.

STAR WARS: JUNIOR JEDI KNIGHTS:
LYRIC'S WORLD

A Berkley Jam Book / published by arrangement with
Lucasfilm Ltd.

PRINTING HISTORY
Boulevard edition / January 1996
Berkley Jam edition / June 1998

The Penguin Putnam Inc. World Wide Web site address is
http://www.penguinputnam.com

Check out the Ace Science Fiction/Fantasy newsletter,
and much more, at Club PPI!

ISBN: 0-425-16762-3

BERKLEY JAM BOOKS®
Berkley Jam Books are published by The Berkley Publishing Group,
a member of Penguin Putnam Inc.,
200 Madison Avenue, New York, New York 10016.
BERKLEY JAM and its logo
are trademarks belonging to Berkley Publishing Corporation.

PRINTED IN THE UNITED STATES OF AMERICA

15   14   13   12   11   10   9   8

For
Susan M. Richardson
(The M stands for my sister; always has.)

PROLOGUE

The purella skittered along the purple rocks that lined a cavern deep within the Sistra mountain. It was almost time again. She knew by the tugging in her ruby red underbelly and the thick strings of yellowed saliva that hung from the four barbed pincers lining her mouth.

Every year at the same time they gathered in the cove for the changing. And every year she found them. It was strange, this hunger she felt for the Melodies, satisfied by gorging on just one of the beings each season. Last year she had pulled a Melodie from the shallow waters, having learned that she could stretch several of her legs far enough to grasp one without falling into the blue-green brine. She did not like water. That was why she never tried to capture an elder. They swam too deep for her. But it didn't matter whether she snared a changeling pulled from the shallow waters, or a being who ringed the cove to protect the others. They all tasted the same.

The purella stopped before a meter-wide crack in the side of the cavern. This would be the place for her web. It was important to have a hidden den, just in case they followed her. And although her eight legs made her roughly two meters wide, her actual body was a bright red bristled mass measuring only one. She could easily fit through the crack. Slowly she crawled up the rocks and sidestepped through the crevice. It was narrow only for a moment, then widened into a darkly lit cave. Her glowing orange eyes surveyed the area. Yes, she thought, this was perfect.

She began to spin her web. Black, sticky, and thick as a rope, it fell in lines behind her as she crisscrossed the cave. As she worked, she thought about the hunt—thought about the Melodie that would soon lie writhing in her gummy snare. The being would not be able to escape, and the more it struggled the more the web would bind, until there would be no movement but the terrified rolling of the Melodie's yellow eyes. That was the moment the purella loved best. When all movement ceased and she was certain of her victory. Certain that the prey could be devoured at her leisure. Yes, she thought happily as she spun, that was the moment she loved best.

ONE

Anakin Skywalker studied the girl in the front row of the Grand Audience Chamber. She sat alone on one of the stone seats that circled the stage. She was a small girl, and he guessed she was about eleven years old. Her long hair cascaded down to her waist in thick red ringlets, and her eyes were a pale yellow color. Anakin had never seen the girl sit with any other candidates. Maybe she was a loner just like he was.

He knew what it felt like to be alone. Anakin had a brother and sister, twins named Jacen and Jaina, and parents, Leia Organa Solo and Han Solo. They all loved him very much, but ever since Anakin could remember, he'd been a loner. Even now that he was a candidate at Luke Skywalker's Jedi academy, surrounded by Jedi students from across the galaxy, he spent a great

3

deal of time alone. It wasn't that he always wanted it that way, it was just that there was so much to think about. Studying to become a Jedi Knight took peace and quiet, something that his new friend, a student at the academy named Tahiri, didn't seem to understand.

Only a week before, Tahiri and Anakin had almost been kicked out of the Jedi academy. They'd snuck away from the academy to raft the river that wound its way through the lush jungles of the moon, Yavin 4. A violent storm had struck. Anakin remembered the broiling green of the river crashing against his body as he and Tahiri shot through the water in a sleek silver raft. His heart skipped a beat as he recalled the look of panic that contorted Tahiri's face when she was thrown from their raft and had to struggle to survive in the cold waters. Without the help of the droid, Artoo-Detoo, he might not have been able to save his friend. If that had happened, he and Tahiri wouldn't have uncovered the evil that lay hidden on Yavin 4 in an ancient palace. An evil that they were now both pledged to destroy.

Anakin heard Tahiri's bare feet padding along the gray stone floor before he saw her. Tahiri was from Tatooine, a desert planet with two scorching suns. Ever since she'd arrived at the academy she'd refused to wear shoes. After living on a hot world filled with gritty sand, Tahiri loved to feel the cool stones of the Great Temple beneath her feet. Anakin's only friend at the academy slid into the seat beside him. She pushed her long blonde hair behind her ears and fixed him with large, green eyes.

Anakin could sense Tahiri's impatience. He knew that she wanted to talk. But Anakin wasn't ready to talk about the evil they'd discovered deep in the jungles of Yavin 4. And he didn't want to discuss the strange creature that had visited his room in the middle of the night. A creature named Ikrit that he'd learned was an ancient Jedi Master. A Master who had drawn both him and Tahiri into the jungles to discover a giant golden globe hidden deep within the crumbling ruins of the Palace of the Woolamander. A crystal sphere created by an evil curse, locked with a riddle, and filled with glittering golden sands and the cries of children trapped within its spell.

Before Anakin could turn to Tahiri to tell her he wasn't ready to talk, Luke Skywalker entered the chamber. Anakin was always amazed by the reaction he felt when his uncle Luke came into a room. The Jedi Master's presence seemed to wash a sense of calm over all of the candidates. Human children and aliens alike stopped shuffling feet, picking through matted black fur, flapping wings.

"May the Force be with you," Luke Skywalker said as his pale blue eyes, almost the same color as his nephew Anakin's, scanned the room. "Today we will begin to learn how to use the Force to travel in our minds to places we have been, but cannot completely remember. In the time you have already spent at the academy, you've learned that training to become a Jedi cannot be taught with words, only with experience. So I won't tell you how to recapture your lost memories. I will say only this: Believe and you succeed. That is part of the Jedi Code, and you must truly accept it if you are to triumph. Are there any questions?"

"What if we fail?" a large, blue-skinned, birdlike alien named Chitter squawked.

Luke Skywalker met Chitter's concerned, beady black eyes with a patient gaze. "Asking the question means that you have already accepted that possibility," he said softly. "Remember, there is no try, only do, for a Jedi. In trying there is success, regardless of the outcome." Luke Skywalker stepped down from the stone stage and quietly left the chamber. The Jedi Knight Tionne, a humanoid woman with silvery hair and mother-of-pearl eyes, walked to the front of the room.

"Please choose partners," Tionne said to the Jedi candidates. Anakin watched as all of the candidates paired with each other. He and Tahiri were partners. Out of the corner of his eye he saw that the girl in the front of the chamber still sat alone.

"Today we are going to learn how to use the Force to travel in our minds to events and places we've experienced before but have difficulty re-calling," Tionne began. "Part of working with the Force is developing the strength of your minds. All of you have heard stories from your childhood of places you've visited and events that took place. But sometimes it's hard to remember things that happened long ago. By using the Force you can reach into the darkest corners of your mind and find memories you can't quite grasp or never knew you had. Work together— this will be a difficult task for most of you."

Anakin turned toward Tahiri, then turned back to look at the red-haired girl. He knew how she must be feeling. He remembered all the times on his home planet, Coruscant, when his older brother and sister had run off to play and left him alone. Quickly he slid off his seat and walked down the aisle to the girl. She was staring at the ground. Slowly she raised her yellow eyes to meet Anakin's blue ones.

"Come join my friend and me," Anakin beck-oned.

The girl quietly stood and followed Anakin back to his seat. She sat down next to Tahiri. "My name is Lyric," the red-haired girl sang out in a voice that sounded like the bubbling of water over the smooth stones of a stream.

"I'm Tahiri, and this is Anakin," Tahiri began chattering. "It's strange that I haven't talked to you before now—I mean, I've talked to just about everyone here. . . . Come to think of it, I tried to speak to you the first day at the academy, after I learned that you'd been here longer than any of us, studying with another group of candidates. You were even shyer than Anakin," Tahiri said with a grin at her friend. "So, where are you from? What planet? You're humanoid, right? How old are you?"

"Tahiri," Anakin said sternly, "give her a chance to answer one question before you shoot another at her." Still, he was pleased that his friend was being so nice to Lyric. Tahiri, too, understood what it was like to be lonely. She was an orphan. Her parents had disappeared when she was three years old, and the Sand People of Tatooine had taken her into their tribe. They were a violent, nomadic race that wore strips of cloth over their entire bodies and dark goggles and breath masks that covered their faces. Tahiri had lived with them for six years. Six years without any contact with other human children.

Tahiri grimaced at Anakin's interruption, then

turned back to Lyric. "So, where are you from?" she asked with a grin.

Lyric met Tahiri's eyes with her large yellow ones. "I am from the moon Yavin 8," she began. "I'm a Melodie."

▥ TWO

The Jedi Knight Tionne walked over to Tahiri, Anakin, and Lyric. "How is your memory work going?" she asked.

Tahiri frowned. She didn't want to do the exercise right now. It was more interesting to learn about Lyric. She'd never met a Melodie before, and she wanted to know more about Yavin 8 and Lyric's species. Tahiri sighed. The conversation would have to wait until later. She smiled at Tionne, then turned to Lyric. "Why don't you tell us a memory that you want to recall?" Tahiri said to the Melodie.

Lyric shyly looked at Tahiri, her large yellow eyes earnest. "Let me think for a moment," she replied, and closed her eyes.

While Anakin waited for Lyric's memory, he began to doodle on a sheet of paper. He was drawing the strange symbols he and Tahiri had seen carved deep in the jungle, in the crumbling stones of the Palace of the Woolamander. Symbols which were not only carved above the entrance to the palace, but deep within its base, down a dark spiral stairway, in the place where Anakin and Tahiri had discovered the mysterious golden globe. In that place, they could almost taste the evil of those who used the Force to serve the dark side.

Anakin forgot about Lyric and Tahiri and closed his eyes, letting himself drift back to the jungle—back one week, when he and Tahiri had rafted the river of Yavin 4 and raced through the rain-soaked jungle to find refuge from the howling winds. Recallingplaces and memories, whether they were recent or far past, was a skill-lhe'd always had. At this very moment, Anakin could smell the dusky sweetness of the Massassi trees that lined the lush moon, could see their dark purplish bark. He could feel the cool soil of the jungle, wet from the storm that had threatened to capsize he and Tahiri's raft.

Anakin moved toward the place he and Tahiri had found to escape the storm, the Palace of the Woolamander, and stood beneath its entrance, staring up through the rain at the strange carvings in its crumbling stones. Then he moved inside the palace and down a dark corridor. He heard the skittering of hundreds of woola-manders as they raced away from his intrusion. Anakin found the crumbling spiral stairway he and Tahiri had descended and slowly dropped into the depths of the palace, to the place where evil coated the stones and called out warnings in a voice laced with danger.

When Anakin reached the base of the steps he stared at the symbols carved in the wall of the small room. Only a week before, he and Tahiri had used the Force to open a hidden passage and reveal the golden globe that had lain in secret for thousands of years. Tahiri had tried to touch the sphere, to break its smooth crystal surface, but a powerful field had thrown her into the stone wall. The globe was untouchable—at least until he and Tahiri could figure out what evil curse surrounded it.

Out of the corner of his eye, Anakin saw Ikrit, the furry white creature he and Tahiri had found sleeping at the base of the globe. He hadn't known then that Ikrit was an ancient Jedi Master who had drawn both him and Tahiri to the globe. Drawn them to break a curse he'd later told them only children, strong in the Force and trained to be Jedi Knights, could break. A curse that no one, not even Luke Skywalker, could know about or help them undo.

13

"Anakin's lost in thought as usual," Tahiri said, breaking his memory.

Lyric smiled softly, then looked over at Anakin. He'd been drawing on a sheet of paper with his eyes closed. She glanced down at the sheet, then drew in her breath sharply.

"What's wrong, Lyric?" Tahiri asked. The girl had gone from pale-skinned to white, and her hands had shot up, covering her eyes with fingers that were linked at their base with pink webs.

"Those symbols," Lyric began.

"What about them?" Anakin asked excitedly. "Have you ever seen them before?" Anakin was certain that understanding the symbols carved in the palace was the next step toward solving the riddle that locked the golden globe. "Do you know what they mean?" he asked Lyric.

"No!" Lyric cried.

"But you recognize them," Tahiri prodded. "You've seen them somewhere before!"

"Yes," Lyric said in a voice that had lost its bubbly quality and now came out in a plaintive gurgle.

"Is it that you can't remember, or that the memory is too frightening?" Anakin said gently. "That's what this exercise is about. We'll help you remember. Please try—it's important."

Lyric closed her eyes and didn't reply. Anakin could sense her torment.

14

"Do you at least remember where you saw the symbols?" Tahiri asked.

"I'd never been off my moon before I came to the academy," Lyric finally said. "It was on Yavin 8."

"Please tell us," Anakin said softly. "Please. It's important."

Lyric looked up and met Anakin's eyes. She steeled herself to remember. To conquer her fear and put into words an experience of terror that she'd blocked from her mind and never spoken of before. "I saw those symbols in the purple granite of my mountain," Lyric began in a faltering voice. She paused, trying to calm herself and let the memory flood back in an icy cold wave. "They were carved beside the nest of a giant avril, and the last time my eyes fell upon their strange design, I was about to be ripped to shreds by the creature's razor-sharp beak."

"What do you mean, ripped to shreds?" Tahiri said with surprise.

"I mean eaten for dinner by a giant bird with a razor-sharp beak and twenty-centimeter talons," Lyric replied. "I was out gathering trico, a plant our young eat, in the tundra below the mountains . . . This will make no sense unless I tell you a bit about my people," Lyric said, interrupting her own story.

"I'm from the species called Melodies. We live deep in the purple mountain named Sistra on the moon Yavin 8," Lyric explained. "Our elders, those who have undergone the changing ceremony, live in pools of crystal blue water that run through much of our city. The children, all those who have yet to change, live around the pools in the caves and caverns of the mountain. It is our job to care for each other, since the elders cannot leave the water, and to watch the eggs—"

"What eggs?" Tahiri interrupted.

"Melodies are humanoid," Lyric reminded Tahiri. "We hatch from eggs spawned by our females. The eggs are kept in a dry cavern within the mountain. When we hatch, we look like human infants. And those of us who haven't changed—who are awaiting our twentieth year, when we are taken to a shallow cove to begin our transformation—care for the young. Part of that care is to gather trico, which is made into a paste to feed our infants until they are old enough to eat the silver-backed fish that we catch in the pools within the mountain.

"When we leave the safety of our home to gather trico," Lyric said, "we travel in groups. Sometimes that isn't enough, though, and the avrils still attack."

"What exactly are avrils?" Anakin asked.

"They're enormous birds of prey with vibrant blue beaks and talons. Their bodies are about two meters long and covered with thick black feathers. When an avril's wings are spread, the span can measure up to eight meters. They feed on raiths, giant black rodents with thick, hairless, green tails; reels, deadly snakes that kill their prey by squeezing the breath out of their bodies; and the purella, a bristle-haired red spider that traps its prey in a thick black web and slowly feeds on it. But their favorite food, by far, is young Melodies. That's why we travel in groups, so that they're less likely to attack. And so that if we come across any of the other predators on our planet, we can fight them together."

Lyric was silent for a moment. She began to recall a memory she visited only in nightmares. "Several years ago, I was gathering trico when we heard the shriek of an attacking avril," Lyric said softly. "There were five of us, and we began to throw the rocks we carry for defense. I can remember the bird's smell, even now. It was sour and dank, and the black feathers that covered its body furrowed as it attacked. We ran out of rocks before the creature tired. And moments later I felt sharp talons wrap around my body and I was airborne. There was nothing the other Melodies could do but fill their sacks with trico and return to the mountains without me. They were certain that I was dead and would soon be devoured by the avril."

"Your friends just let the avril fly away with you?" Tahiri said in shock.

"Yes," Lyric replied, her eyes wide with remembered terror. "There was nothing they could do."

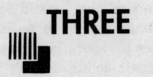 **THREE**

"They didn't abandon me," Lyric hastened to say as she saw the identical looks of horror on the faces of her new friends. "One of the reasons the elders allowed me to come to the Jedi academy is because the children of my people do not know how to defend themselves well from predators, and the adults cannot leave the water to help us survive. It was the elders' hope that I might learn to use the Force to help my people," Lyric explained.

"But I am getting ahead of my story. The avril who attacked my group and snatched me took me to her nest, a shallow hole in the mountains, high above my own home. I heard her young squawking for food as I was dropped before their unseeing newborn eyes in a nest of twigs and trico. As I lay on my back, I saw the same type of symbols as

Anakin drew. I did not have long to wonder how or when the carvings had been made. But I could tell they were created from the hand of an intelligent being.

"The avril towered above me; I could see its black tongue lashing back and forth as it prepared to devour me, later to regurgitate me in the way these birds feed their young. I don't know why I did it, but I began to squawk back at the creature. I tried to make my voice sound like the very same cries as the young that surrounded me. The avril began to hop madly. I could sense its confusion. Then, in a whirl of feathers, it flew off. I can only assume that I copied the cries of the creature's young so well that it thought I was one of them and went off to find more food. I scrambled down the rocky mountain, desperate to find my way back home. Several hours later, battered but alive, I entered the portal to my city."

Lyric paused and looked at Anakin and Tahiri. "I wish I could tell you more about the symbols I saw, because it is obviously terribly important to both of you," she said sadly. "But all I can tell you is that they are much like the ones Anakin drew. That is all I know."

"Are there others on your moon who might know?" Anakin asked.

"Perhaps the old ones," Lyric replied. "But they

no longer surface, so I have never spoken to them."

Anakin and Tahiri both frowned. They desperately needed to figure out what the symbols carved above the palace meant if they had any hope of solving the riddle of the golden globe.

"Why do the elder Melodies live in water?" Tahiri asked.

"After the changing, our bodies can no longer survive outside the water. We develop gills and breathe by extracting oxygen from water. In addition, we can no longer walk on land because our legs fuse into a large webbed tail," Lyric said. "Most of the elders can surface for varying amounts of time, which they do to see their young and give us guidance. However, the very old cannot surface at all."

"Let me get this straight," Tahiri gasped. "You're telling us that you're going to turn into a fish?"

Anakin scowled at Tahiri. Sometimes she could be rude!

"Not exactly," Lyric said, laughing. "Our upper body remains about the same, but our ability to breathe, as well as the form of our lower body, changes."

"What is the changing like?" Anakin asked. He had sensed deep fear beneath Lyric's lighthearted laugh.

"Seldom do all of us survive," Lyric replied softly. "Very seldom. I leave tomorrow morning for Yavin 8 . . . for my changing. That is why I was at the academy before you arrived, Tahiri," Lyric explained. "My time to study the Force is limited."

When it was time for the candidates to leave the Grand Audience Chamber, Lyric hung back. "Go ahead, I'll meet up with you later," she called to her new friends. They hesitated. "Please go," Lyric said softly. Anakin and Tahiri both saw that thick salty tears were on the brink of spilling from Lyric's eyes. They left the chamber and waited for their new friend in the corridor.

The Jedi Knight Tionne walked over to Lyric and sat on a stone seat by her side. "I don't want to go," Lyric cried to Tionne. "Tomorrow I'll be sent back to Yavin 8 when the supply shuttle leaves. I'll be taken to the cove where the others who were born at the same time as me will be waiting for the changing, just below the blue-green algae that covers the surface of the waters in the cove. And while I'm changing, I'll be defenseless," Lyric wailed.

Tionne knew all too well what Lyric was going to face. She'd been to Yavin 8 during her search for Jedi candidates for the academy, and had witnessed a changing ceremony. Tionne recalled the explanation Lyric had given her months before, when she'd questioned why the Melodies had to partake in a ceremony set in such a dangerous place. The shallow algae-covered waters of the cove were the only place on the mountain where the changing could occur. Until the changing was complete, the young Melodies needed the blue-green algae that carpeted the waters and created oxygen through photosynthesis, to provide them with enough oxygen to breathe.

Once their gill slits were completely formed, the Melodies would be able to extract oxygen from water without the help of the algae and could be moved to safety—to the deep pool of water within the mountain. Until that time, Melodie children did their best to protect the changelings. The children circled the shallow cove and sat on its banks with bags of rocks to fight off the purella, avrils, reels, and raiths that came to feed on the changing Melodies. Those creatures seemed to instinctively know the right season to hunt for changelings, Tionne grimly recalled.

Lyric had ringed the cove with the other children for many seasons of changing ceremonies. She knew all too well, Tionne thought, that though the children always fought without fear for their lives, some of the changelings as well as some of the children didn't survive the day.

"I don't want to go," Lyric said plaintively. "I want to stay at the academy."

Tionne studied the young Melodie. From what she'd seen, Lyric was more than ready for the changing. In the past few weeks, she'd noticed that the child had begun to have difficulty breathing, her breaths sometimes sounding like rattling, dry gasps.

"Lyric, do you remember when I fought by your side at the cove?" Tionne asked.

Lyric nodded. "You came in search of Jedi candidates, but it was the day of the changing, and you fought to help save those who would become elders," she whispered. "I remember an avril swooped over your head and tried to slash you with its sharp talons, and you didn't see the reel that slithered up behind you," Lyric said.

"You saw the thick violet snake moments before it wrapped me in its coils and began to hiss and squeeze," Tionne said softly. "I recall that you turned and, without thought, stared into its black eyes and began to hiss at the long creature. Lyric, your voice, the voice of rushing streams and tinkling water, became the snake's voice. Just as I was about to be crushed, the creature released me from its coils and slithered away. For that reason, I took you to study at the Jedi academy.

"You were strong in the Force, even then," Tionne said to her student. "You are even stronger now. But if you don't return to Yavin 8 and undergo the changing, you'll die. You knew

24

that you wouldn't have a lot of time at the academy," Tionne continued. "You said that you wanted to study here anyway, in the hopes that you could use your training to help your people when you returned to Yavin 8. If you want to help them, you must return. And you must survive."

Slowly Lyric turned and left the room. Tionne was right, she thought. The only way to help her people learn to fight and survive was to teach them what she had learned at the academy. To find other Melodies who were sensitive to the Force, and train them to use their voices and minds to fight the predators that fed on the Melodies' eggs and changelings. Still, her sobs caught in her throat as she left the Grand Audience Chamber.

"Lyric," Tahiri called out. "We didn't mean to eavesdrop, but we were worried about you. How can we help?" she asked.

Lyric shook her head. "You can't," she answered sadly. "This is something I have to do alone."

"Why?" Anakin asked suddenly. "Why can't Tahiri and I go with you to Yavin 8 and help you through the changing ceremony?"

"Your place is at the academy," Lyric murmured.

"Our place is with our friend," Tahiri replied.

FOUR

The battered supply ship, the *Lightning Rod,* slid silently through the morning sky. Its courier and message runner—a longhaired pilot named Peckhum—navigated the ship past Yavin's moons. Old Peckhum would not only take Anakin, Tahiri, and Lyric to Yavin 8, but would accompany them throughout their journey. Lyric's world was too dangerous a place for the children to be alone.

Anakin and Tahiri sat side by side. Anakin stared out his window. As they passed Yavin 13, he found himself wondering about the moon. It was said to be inhabited by reptilian creatures called slith. He'd read that the slith were meat-eating creatures with enormous jaws lined with spiked teeth. Anakin shook off his thoughts and rose from his seat to check on Lyric, who was sitting up front with Old Peckhum. Since they'd left the academy, she hadn't spoken. And, while Anakin knew that she was relieved to have him and Tahiri with her, he could also sense her apprehension and fear.

Persuading Luke Skywalker to allow them to accompany their friend to Yavin 8 had been difficult. Anakin thought about the conversation they'd had that morning with his uncle.

"She needs us!" Tahiri had cried. "Please let us go to Yavin 8 with Lyric. Anakin and I can help her survive her changing, I know we can! And Peckhum will be there to protect us."

Luke Skywalker had been unmoved. "I can't send students into a potentially hazardous situation," he had said.

"Uncle Luke, you're the one who said that we can't learn to become Jedi Knights by listening to words. Experience is the best teacher, right?" Anakin had asked innocently, his ice blue eyes meeting his uncle's pale ones. "Please let us help Lyric." Finally, Luke Skywalker had agreed.

Anakin stared out the window as the supply shuttle sped through the silent sky. He thought about that morning. As he'd packed his academy jumpsuit and some extra socks, Ikrit, the Jedi Master they'd found in the palace, had climbed through the open window of his room.

"Where are you going, young Anakin?" Ikrit had asked in his raspy voice.

Anakin had explained the situation. "Are we wrong to leave now, when we haven't solved the riddle of the golden globe?" Anakin asked.

Ikrit had only replied, "You must go where you are needed. You must go where you are drawn." Then the Master had swung off the window ledge and scampered down the pyramid-shaped stone wall of the Great Temple.

Anakin hadn't expected him to be much help. Ikrit had already explained that if an adult Jedi Knight or Master tried to break the curse, the globe would shatter into a thousand pieces of crystal. Anakin understood that he and Tahiri were on their own. His thoughts were interrupted.

"Anakin, have you thought much about the globe?" Tahiri whispered. She didn't wait for an answer. "I have. I don't know how, but we've got to understand what the symbols carved in the palace and in the mountain on Lyric's planet mean. It's the only way I can think to figure out how to break the curse."

The curse. Ikrit had come to Anakin's room the night he'd returned from the Palace of the Woolamander. He'd explained to Anakin that four hundred years ago he'd discovered the globe in the ruins of the palace, which had been built thou-

29

sands of years earlier by an ancient race called the Massassi. Ikrit said that he couldn't break the curse, so he'd curled up at the base of the globe to wait for the people who could. Those people were Anakin and Tahiri. When Anakin had told Tahiri what Ikrit had said, she'd agreed that they had to work together to break into the crystal sphere that was locked with a riddle and filled with glittering golden sands and the cries of trapped Massassi children.

"I think you're right," Anakin said to Tahiri now. "Understanding what the Massassi wrote in their palace will help us to unravel the riddle of the globe. But right now, we've got to concentrate on helping Lyric." He didn't add that he'd seen Ikrit. Or tell Tahiri Ikrit's words. It was enough to feel that what he and Tahiri were doing was right. And to know that he felt drawn both to Lyric and her moon.

The shuttle dipped toward Yavin 8. Anakin watched the moon grow in size as they sped toward its surface. He could see that it was covered with brown and green tundra and a ridge of purple mountains that jutted from its surface. Moments later, the ship gently touched down, only a few hundred meters from the mountains. Lyric moved back to join her friends. In the time of the flight, her breathing had become alarmingly labored. It escaped from her mouth in deep rattles and hisses, and Anakin could see that the effort of drawing air was exhausting her. Lyric raised one hand to brush her red ringlets from her eyes. Anakin gasped. In the last hour, the pink webs on her hands had spread until they reached the tips of her fingers. It was clearly getting close to the time for her changing ceremony.

The silver door of the shuttle hissed open. Old Peckhum, Anakin, and Tahiri followed their friend down the ramp. Waiting for them were five Melodie children. "Welcome," one of the Melodies began, but he stopped when he saw Lyric. "Come," he said, "we've got to get Lyric to the cove quickly." The look of worry on his face told Anakin all he needed to know. He reached up and took hold of Lyric's elbow. Tahiri moved to the other side, and together they helped Lyric half walk, half run to the mountains that loomed before them.

"Oh no!" Peckhum cried as he followed the children toward the mountain.

"What is it?" Anakin asked as he ran.

"I forgot some of the supplies I need to transport after we leave Yavin 8," Peckhum worriedly explained. "It wouldn't be important, except they're medical supplies, and this trip has already put me behind schedule."

"Go back and get them," Anakin called over his shoulder. "You'll only be gone for a few hours, and we'll be fine. Just come find us in the mountains when you return."

"I don't think I should leave you. Luke Skywalker wouldn't be pleased," Peckhum said uncertainly.

"Don't worry," Anakin replied. "He'll understand." He stopped, and turned to Peckhum. "We'll be careful."

"All right," Peckhum said. "But don't get into any trouble while I'm gone." He turned and raced back to the *Lightning Rod*. Moments later he shot into the sky and disappeared from view. Anakin ran to catch up with his friends.

Barely a moment later, the ear-shattering shriek of an avril rolled down over the group. Anakin didn't have to ask what creature had made the sound. He felt its enormous shadow fall across his back before he looked up to see blood red talons slashing down toward the group. The Melodies quickly formed a circle and began to heave stones up at the creature. Several hit, but only maddened the black bird. Tahiri grabbed a large rock and threw it, hard. Her shot struck the avril directly between the eyes. It shrieked in anger and dove toward her, beak open, talons outstretched. Tahiri dodged, but not before one of its massive wings struck and threw her meters away from the group.

Anakin raced over to protect his friend. But he

wasn't quick enough. The avril dove toward Tahiri, talons outstretched, its scream of attack mingling with her cry of terror. Anakin was too far away to reach her, and dread washed over him in an icy cold wave. A split second before Tahiri was swept away in the avril's hungry grasp, Lyric, who was closest to her, leapt forward. She threw her body over Tahiri's to shield her friend. The avril sank his talons into the orange academy jumpsuit Lyric wore, and shot toward the sky. Lyric hung limply in the air.

All who stood helpless on the tundra of the moon could see the look of terror on Lyric's face as she was borne away.

 # FIVE

"Where is it taking her?" Tahiri cried. Both she and Anakin whirled to face the Melodies.

"There is nothing to be done," one of the young boys said sadly. "It will take her to its nest and she will be gone before we can ever reach it."

"But she's survived before," Anakin said.

"Yes, but this time she is too weak, she is ready for the changing. If she is not in the waters of the cove before sunrise, she will die," the boy replied.

"Where's the nest?" Anakin asked in a voice that couldn't be argued with. The boy pointed to a spot halfway up the mountain, and Anakin and Tahiri immediately raced toward it. "Be here when we return to take us to the cove," Anakin called over his shoulder.

They'd been climbing for over an hour. Anakin could hear the rasp of his breath, the thundering of his heart. Tahiri was right behind him. She, too, was gasping. There was less oxygen in the air because of the altitude, and several times Anakin had felt dizzy, felt black walls threatening to close out his consciousness, and he'd turned around to make sure Tahiri was still on her feet. They didn't speak as they climbed. Instead they focused on the dark hole where the young Melodie had pointed. Believe and you succeed, Anakin thought as he climbed. That was part of the Jedi Code. Anakin repeated it over and over in his head. He saw the purplish rocks beneath his scraped hands begin to lighten as dawn threatened to cover the moon in its soft glow. Anakin climbed faster.

They stopped five meters from the entrance to the avril's nest. Anakin could hear the creature shrieking within the shallow cave. He and Tahiri crept forward, trying not to dislodge any rocks. They didn't want the bird to know they were there. Carefully they moved toward the opening, peeking around rocks until they were directly below the cave. Anakin raised himself up slowly and peered into the dimly lit cavern. He smelled the foul air and heard the rustling and chirping of the creature's chicks before his eyes grew used to the cave. Then he saw Lyric.

She was alive. Her body hung over the edge of the avril's nest, ringlets of red hair reaching down to the ground. As she had done before, she was chirping, trying to sound like the mottled black chicks around her. Anakin could hear Lyric struggling for the breath she needed to make the noises. She could barely gasp out the sounds. Still, her efforts had been enough to confuse the creature, whose black head was cocked to one side as it towered above her. But Lyric's efforts were not enough to send the avril out looking for more food. Anakin crouched back down and crawled over to Tahiri.

"I've got to go in there," Anakin mouthed to his friend. A look of alarm spread across Tahiri's features. "I'm going to try to get the avril to leave her nest to search for more food."

"I'm going too," Tahiri mouthed back.

"No, stay hidden in the rocks. I might need your help, or Lyric might. It won't do us any good if the avril attacks us both," Anakin whispered furiously.

"I don't like this," Tahiri mouthed with a scowl.

Anakin turned and crept back up to the nest. Then he let out a shriek. The avril burst out of the cave and loomed above him, her beak open wide in an ear-shattering cry. Anakin stood fast and shrieked again, in what he hoped was the sound of one of the creature's chicks. He saw the bird's beady eyes boring down on him. And when the avril rushed forward, he was struck by foul, sour air. With a swift motion, the bird grasped him in its beak and flung him into her nest. Anakin curled into a ball next to the chicks and continued to shriek. The avril began to hop from foot to foot, wings flapping in distress.

That's right, Anakin thought, I'm not dinner. Go out and find some food for your hungry babies. Lyric continued to chirp and attempted a shriek, but her lungs couldn't sustain the effort. Then, with a sudden burst, the avril left her nest and soared away from the mountain.

"Anakin, are you all right?" Tahiri called as she scrambled to the opening of the cave.

"I'm fine," Anakin replied. "But Lyric's in bad shape. We've got to get her out of here."

Tahiri wrinkled her nose as the thick, dank smell of the cave struck her. Then she climbed into the nest and began to help Anakin lift Lyric.

"Leave me," Lyric gasped. "It's too late. Save yourselves. The avril will be back soon."

"There is no try, only do," Tahiri muttered under her breath as she hoisted one of Lyric's arms over her shoulders. Anakin lifted the other one. As they dragged their friend from the avril's nest, both Anakin and Tahiri saw the symbols carved in the purple rocks. "This is the same place she was taken before," Tahiri gasped in surprise.

"We'd better hurry," Anakin said. They quickly left the cave and began the journey down the mountain. At times Lyric tried to take a step or two, but her efforts didn't last long. Any movement made it too difficult for her to breathe. Finally, Anakin hoisted Lyric onto his back. He listened to her wheezing breaths in his ear as he carried her. Tahiri scrambled down the rocks in front of him, then helped him keep his balance as he climbed down. They were running out of time. Suddenly they heard the maddened scream of the avril overhead.

"Over here," a boy's voice called. Anakin saw the young Melodie he'd told to wait. With renewed energy, he moved quickly over to the boy. Several more Melodies were waiting, and they lifted Lyric off Anakin's back and carried her through a small hole in the rocks. The avril landed by the hole and shrieked angrily. It was too small for her to follow her prey. Anakin, Tahiri, and the Melodies heard the creature scraping at the rocks with her talons. Her scrapes and cries faded into the distance as the group raced through a tunnel in the mountain.

Anakin and Tahiri followed the Melodies. The tunnel within the purple mountain of Sistra wound deep, and just when Anakin began to fear that Lyric would run out of time before they reached the cove, the afternoon light began to pour over the group. They reached an opening, and before them was a circular area, roughly ten meters round, filled with water that was blanketed with blue-green algae. The Melodies who carried Lyric moved toward the edge of the pool and gently slid Lyric in. She floated on the bed of algae for a moment, then slowly sank beneath it and disappeared from view.

Tahiri and Anakin stared at the blue-green pool of water. It rippled with movement from beneath its surface. Anakin turned and studied the cove. It was set deep within the mountain, but the jagged rocks that ringed it did not close out the sky. The entire cove was open to a shaft of thick sunlight. Perched on the rocks surrounding the pool were young Melodies with bagfuls of stones.

"She'll be all right now," one of the Melodies said in a voice that sounded like the soft patter of water falling on dry sand. "You brought her in time."

SIX

Anakin took the bag of stones and sharp spear that one of the Melodies held out to him. Then he moved to a flat rock next to the spot where Lyric had disappeared and crouched, ready to defend his friend. Anakin hoped that he could help protect Lyric and the other changelings by using the Force, but if not, he'd use the weapons that rested at his feet. Tahiri, too, was given a sack of stones and a spear. Anakin looked at his friend. Her orange jumpsuit was covered with purplish smudges of dirt from the mountains, and dust streaked her white blonde hair. Tahiri met Anakin's ice blue eyes. Her own green ones flashed. She, too, was determined to protect their friend.

Suddenly a young girl raced into the sunlight of

the cove. "The eggs!" the girl cried. "They're attacking the eggs!"

Anakin felt the terror of the girl's voice cut through him like a lightsaber. He jumped to his feet. "Stay here and watch out for Lyric," he called to Tahiri. Then he raced to the tunnel behind two Melodies. They tore through the dark passageways. Anakin felt the raiths before he saw them. He sensed their hunger, their frenzied aggression. The group rounded a corner, rocks poised. Before them was a large cavern stacked with pure white eggs. And in its center were three enormous black rodents, their thick, hairless, green tails lashing madly as they faced the two young female Melodies who stood between them and the eggs. The girls stood, rocks ready to throw. The Melodies beside Anakin didn't budge. They were frozen by their own fear.

"Don't move," Anakin called softly to the girls. The creatures were too large to be killed with mere stones. Once the Melodies began their attack, the rodents would be on them. The girls wouldn't survive, Anakin thought. Anakin moved between the Melodies and stood directly behind the raiths, spear poised. The loathsome rodents heard him approach and turned. They reared on massive haunches and snarled. On their hind legs, they stood a full three meters. Anakin

42

watched thick brown saliva drip from their pointed teeth.

A steady calm washed over Anakin, and he opened himself to the Force. He could feel the beating of the rodents' hearts, feel the air rustle as their black whiskers twitched.

"Did you think I was going to let you have all the fun?" a soft voice whispered as Tahiri joined Anakin. She held her spear before her. "Let them attack first," Tahiri said quietly. "If they're anything like the womp rats on Tatooine, you'll be able to sense which way they'll strike a split second before they—"

Tahiri's explanation was cut short as one of the raiths emitted a high-pierced whine and launched itself. She ducked sideways, keeping her spear vertical. The raith impaled itself on the sharp tip. Tahiri hardly noticed the thick green blood that sprang from the wound. She wrenched her spear out of the dead creature and turned to face the other two rodents.

Anakin moved with one graceful motion as a raith leapt toward him, its teeth gnashing. He rolled forward and met the creature with his spear midair. It screamed in anger and pain, then fell in a crumple to the floor.

"Anakin, watch out!" Tahiri cried. Anakin lunged sideways as the third raith flew toward him. He had not had time to pull his spear out of the one he'd just fought. Now, weaponless, he stood facing a snarling raith, driven mad by the death of its companions and its own hunger and frustration. He could feel the rodent's hot, rancid breath on his face, and he crouched in readiness to spring sideways when the beast attacked.

"Hey, big guy, over here," Tahiri called out from behind the raith. It twisted and sprung at her in one powerful movement. Tahiri was ready, and seconds later the rodent lay twitching at her feet. For a moment the cavern was filled with silence. The pure white eggs almost seemed to glow around them.

"We'd better get back to the cove," Anakin finally said. The Melodies nodded, then led the two Jedi candidates through the tunnels. All was quiet when they entered the light of the cove.

"How did you fight the raiths so well?" one of the Melodies asked Anakin once he was settled on a rock by the pool. "We have been fighting them all our lives," the girl added. "But never like that."

Anakin met her questioning gaze. "What is your name?" he asked.

"Sannah," the girl replied. The Melodie looked about nine years old, Anakin thought. He wondered how old she really was. Her white forehead was furrowed in concentration as she gazed intently at Anakin with yellow eyes ringed with thick, brown lashes.

"Sannah, do you know what the Force is?" he began. She shook her head. "It's an energy field generated by all living things. It surrounds everything, and binds the galaxy together. At the Jedi academy we learn to feel that field, to control, sense, and alter it. The skills we develop also help us to sense emotions. Tahiri and I used our abilities to feel the raiths' anger, to sense their movements at the split second before they made them. By doing that, we could anticipate where they would strike."

"And if I want to learn these things?" Sannah said softly. "If I want to learn how to fight so that I can protect my people?"

Anakin stared into the girl's yellow eyes. It was clear that she desperately wanted to be of help. But he also sensed her anger. Sannah had obviously lost many she loved to the predators on her planet. How could he help her to understand?

"The Force is meant to be used for peace, knowledge, and serenity. Using it in anger will lead to the dark side, a place where the Force is used for evil," Anakin began. "There was once a man named Darth Vader who used the Force to help destroy the Jedi Knights and create an Empire designed to rule through aggression and corruption. His real name was Anakin Skywalker, and he was my grandfather." The young Melodie gasped.

"My uncle, the Jedi Master Luke Skywalker, created the Jedi academy to help fill the galaxy again with Jedi Knights who are pledged to defend good against evil," Anakin explained. "But he teaches us about Darth Vader and all the other evil men and women who used the Force in anger and aggression. By learning about them, we can protect ourselves from following in their footsteps, because the lure of the dark side can be powerful."

"Does it frighten you to be named after an evil man?" Sannah asked innocently.

"Sometimes," Anakin said softly. For a moment he could hear the dark voices that rose from the spiral stairway in the Palace of the Woolamander. Voices that told him he was just like his grandfather, and goaded him to use the Force to strike out in anger. Voices dripping with menace and warning that whoever tried to break through the field surrounding the golden globe would fail, would die. He shrugged off the memory as he flung thick brown bangs from his eyes.

"Do you know anything about the strange symbols carved in the rock walls of Sistra?" Anakin asked Sannah.

"Yes," she replied matter-of-factly. "Some of us have seen carvings in the mountains. They're in the lower tunnels and several of the caverns and caves. Some say they're a message from an ancient race."

"Do you think they're right?" Anakin asked.

"Yes, I think they are," Sannah replied.

SEVEN

"How many changelings are there?" Tahiri asked the girl who crouched beside Anakin.

Sannah stared down at the pool. "Lyric is one of a spawned group of seven," she replied.

"How do you know if they're all right down there?" Tahiri asked with a nod at the pool. Except for a few ripples and splashes, the water remained calm.

"We check on them every few hours," Sannah explained.

"But if you're not a changeling or an elder, how can you breathe underwater?" Anakin said in surprise.

Sannah pulled several long rectangles of green material from a pocket on the tunic she wore. "We weave this material out of the stems of the trico plant," Sannah said. "Then we sew it together to form a large pocket. We pack the pocket with the blue-green algae that floats on top of the pool, and tie it over our nose and mouth. The trico repels water, and the algae allows us to breathe oxygen beneath the surface for several minutes."

"Can we go see Lyric?" Anakin asked.

"Er, Anakin, have you forgotten that I can't swim?" Tahiri whispered.

Anakin hadn't forgotten. He'd never forget watching Tahiri struggle beneath the waters of the river on Yavin 4. He'd never forget that she'd almost drowned. "Tahiri, one of us has to stay on the surface to help the Melodies fight if any predators attack," Anakin said. "So if it's all right with you, I'll go see Lyric."

"It's all right with me," Tahiri said in a relieved voice.

Sannah helped Anakin scoop algae out of the pool and pack it into the trico filter. "It may be difficult for you to breathe at first," Sannah warned. "Until your body relaxes and gets used to breathing oxygen from the algae, you will try to struggle for air. Once the filter is on, sit for a moment before you enter the water."

Anakin lifted up the filter and Sannah helped him tie it. He moved toward a rock and sat down. He realized he was holding his breath, and slowly exhaled. However, when he went to inhale, his lungs struggled to pull in air, struggled for the type of oxygen they'd always processed. Anakin felt a dull pounding in his ears, and his vision blurred. I'm not going to pass out, he instructed himself. He forced himself to remain calm, to inhale and exhale. Moments later he was breathing the oxygen from the algae. Tahiri's concerned face came into view. Anakin reassured his friend with his ice blue eyes. Then he moved to the edge of the algae pool and slipped in.

It took several moments to adjust to the murky water below the surface. The algae filtered out most of the sunlight from above, and only narrow shafts of light lit his way. Anakin swam through the water, breathing shallowly and searching for his friend. The pool was roughly two meters deep, and he passed several changeling forms in the water. They all wore the same pale green tunic that Sannah wore.

As he swam, Anakin noticed that most of the changelings still had partial legs, although they were beginning to fuse together with thick webs striped with pale blue, green, orange, and pink. The Melodies didn't take notice of him as he passed them. They slowly rolled in the water as the currents sent from his movement washed over them, but their eyes were closed. It was almost as if they were asleep. Anakin had still not seen Lyric.

A flash of orange caught Anakin's eye. He

moved through the bodies toward his friend, still dressed in her academy jumpsuit. He reached Lyric and saw that she, too, was sleeping. Her jumpsuit now hung in tatters around her legs as they fused together and broke the seams that had once made pant legs. Thick red hair floated around her still face. Anakin almost let out a cry as Lyric suddenly opened her yellow eyes and met his gaze. She must have sensed his presence, he thought. Lyric's look told Anakin what he needed to know: she was all right. And she knew that he and Tahiri were still there protecting her. Slowly Lyric closed her eyes. Anakin reached over and held her hand. He would stay with her until his oxygen began to run out.

Something was wrong! Anakin wasn't certain if he'd heard Tahiri cry or if he'd sensed her fear. Gently releasing Lyric's hand, he shot through the murky waters and burst through the blanket of algae. It covered his eyes in thick strands, and for a moment he was blinded. Then he saw it. An enormous reel, deep violet in color, was hissing furiously before Tahiri, who stood between the snake and the pool of water.

"Throw me a spear!" Tahiri cried over to a Melodie. But the young boy couldn't seem to move. He was terrified. "Throw me a spear!" Tahiri yelled again. The snake's black forked tongue flicked toward Tahiri. It was tasting its prey.

Anakin could sense the frustration and fear in Tahiri's cry. Sannah tried to move to grab a spear for Tahiri, but at her movement the snake turned as if to strike her, and she shrank back. "I'm right behind you, Tahiri," Anakin called softly.

"Wish you were in front of me," Tahiri called back. " 'Cause I'm not sure how to fight this thing. I tried to copy its hissing, like Lyric did to save Tionne, but it doesn't seem to like my voice." In a lightning strike, the snake leapt at Tahiri. She sprang sideways and it just missed grasping her in its thick coils. Tahiri lay sprawled on her back as the reel circled its prey. When it struck again, she rolled sideways. This time it didn't circle, but lashed out immediately. Tahiri couldn't get to her feet fast enough to evade the serpentine creature. Instantly she was trapped within half-meter-thick violet coils. "Help me, Anakin!" Tahiri screamed. "It's crushing me!"

The Melodies around the cove came to life and began to pummel the reel with their rocks. Several attempted to stab it with spears, but their weapons fell to the ground, unable to pierce the creature's thick scales. It seemed impervious to attack, and continued to constrict around Tahiri's body. "Anakin!" Tahiri gasped.

Anakin leapt out of the water, grabbed a spear,

and launched himself onto the reel. He stood on the creature's slick body and tried to stab through its thick scales. With a sharp crack, his spear broke in two. The reel began to roll, bearing down on Tahiri. Anakin was tossed to the rocks. There are all kinds of strength, he thought as he got to his feet. He could see Tahiri's face, barely visible within the snake's coils. It was a face contorted with pain. Soon, the reel would crush her.

Anakin closed his eyes. He reached out with the Force and pried into the snake's body. The creature was cold-blooded, and Anakin immediately felt chilled. He felt the reel's cartilage, its muscles, even the beating of the creature's heart. He focused on the heart. Focused on slowing its beat. He felt the constricting coils begin to relax, to loosen. Slower, slower, slower, he thought, until he opened his eyes, startled. The heart had stopped completely.

Tahiri lay in the relaxed coils of the dead reel. Anakin climbed over rows of coils to his friend. "Tahiri, are you all right?" he asked.

Slowly Tahiri opened her eyes. She'd passed out from the grip of the snake. She stared at Anakin, not comprehending. Then her eyes grew wide and she let out a cry.

"It's all right," Anakin said as he helped her throw off a thick violet coil and stand up. "Are you okay?"

"Feels like one of my ribs might be cracked," Tahiri said with a grimace of pain. "But other than that, I'm fine." She gave Anakin a little smile. "How'd you get it to let me go?" she asked.

"My spear wasn't any use, so I closed my eyes and used the Force," Anakin explained. "I found its heart and focused on slowing it to weaken the snake. I guess I slowed it so much that it stopped, and the reel died." Anakin fell silent. He was surprised at his own power.

Sannah walked up to the two Jedi candidates. "I don't understand how you defeated the reel, but we are thankful. Tonight," she said with a grin at the dead snake at their feet, "we will all eat well."

EIGHT

The thick shaft of sunlight that had glanced off the algae on the top of the pool began to fade. The rocks surrounding the cove of water darkened into a rich purple hue. Young Melodies still perched around the pool, rocks and spears in hand. Since the reel died, the cove had been quiet. One of the Melodies tied on a filter and slipped into the pool. "It is done," he cried as he resurfaced.

The Melodies moved down from the rocks and gathered by the pool. The changelings surfaced one by one, still groggy from their metamorphosis. Hands pulled each from the waters, revealing shimmering tails striped with blue, green, purple, pink, and orange. The changelings were carried back into the tunnels of the mountain.

"Where are they taking them?" Tahiri worriedly asked Sannah.

"They have changed," Sannah replied. "They are being taken to the crystal waters where the elders live. But we must move them quickly— they are still very weak and can't be out of the water for too long."

Anakin and Tahiri stood breathlessly at the edge of the pool. Lyric hadn't emerged yet. Then Anakin saw Lyric's bright red hair. She swam slowly to the side of the pool and allowed a group of Melodies to pull her from the waters. Her orange jumpsuit had disappeared, and her body was completely changed. Where her legs had been, a shimmering, multicolored fish tail now appeared. Several long gill slits lined her ribs, and her fingers were now completely attached by glistening pick webs. Lyric smiled weakly at her friends as they helped carry her through the mountain.

The passageway they traveled wound up into the mountain. The Melodies carried the changelings carefully, half running through the steep tunnels. Then suddenly their pace slowed. "Why are we stopping?" Anakin called out to the group in front of him.

"Raith," was the frightened reply.

Anakin and Tahiri gently put Lyric on the rocks, then raced past the group of Melodies in

front of them. They ran down the tunnel, following the stricken cries of a male Melodie. As the
tunnel veered left, they stopped short. The raith
had already bitten one of the Melodies. The boy
lay wounded, but alive. Now the foul creature
crouched on its haunches, snarling at the female
Melodie that had moved to stand between it and
the boy it had wounded. It was Sannah.

"Sannah, don't move!" Anakin cried. But his
warning was too late. The giant black rodent gave
a throaty growl and launched toward the young
girl, teeth bared. She dove sideways, flipping in
the air, and landed on her feet. The infuriated
raith charged again. This time Sannah whirled
sideways, spear raised. The sharp tip glanced off
the raith's flank, and it whined at the burning
pain. But it wasn't a mortal wound and the creature turned again, thick brown threads of drool
flying from its jaws as it snarled at Sannah.
When it charged again, Sannah leapt back, and
the raith's jagged teeth snapped on thin air.
Then, using the split second the creature took to
regain its balance, Sannah charged. Her spear
ran straight through the belly of the raith. The
massive black rodent fell dead at her feet.

"You used the Force, didn't you?" Anakin asked
Sannah, breaking the awed hush of the room.

Sannah turned toward Anakin, still breathless

from her battle. "I don't know how I did it," she replied. "I just felt it."

"You did it well," Anakin said with a small smile. Then he turned and followed Tahiri back to Lyric, whom they helped the young Melodies lift. The tunnel curled upward for several more minutes, then suddenly ended. It emptied out into an enormous cavern filtered with light from small holes in the sides and top of the rocks. The late-afternoon sun played off the deep crystal blue waters in the center of the chamber. The Melodies moved to the side of the waters that gently lapped at the rocks. They slid the changelings into the liquid darkness. Then the elders surfaced and called their greetings to the children. Their bodies moved swiftly along the surface of the water as their hands reached for the changelings, held them as parents embrace their children. Children who are finally home.

Anakin and Tahiri watched as the elders celebrated the changing of their young. They leapt into the air and twisted and somersaulted before diving back down into the waters again. They splashed delightedly, their tails shimmering. Several elders perched at the edge of the pool and spoke with the children who had not yet been changed. They caught up on what had happened, eyed the Jedi candidates, and offered shy smiles. Anakin sensed that the elders yearned for the day when the next changelings would come safely into their depths. Because until that moment, they couldn't truly protect their young.

"Will they be safe now?" Tahiri asked Sannah when she came over to speak to her and Anakin.

"Yes," Sannah said with a sweet smile. "They are safe in the high waters. The raiths and the purella cannot swim, and the reels do not come this high in the mountain," she explained.

"Anakin, Tahiri," a voice bubbled from the waters. Lyric floated behind the Jedi candidates. She smiled happily at them, and swam to the side of the pool. "Thank you," Lyric said. "I have heard how you fought the raiths and a reel. Are you okay, Tahiri?" she said with concern.

"I'm fine," Tahiri replied.

"You saved not only my life, but the lives of several other Melodies," Lyric said. "The elders wish to reward you for your bravery. They asked me what would be suitable, and I suggested that you be allowed to come beneath the surface of these waters to speak with an old one who we call the keeper of legends. He may know something about your strange symbols. Would you like to do that?" Lyric asked.

"Would we?" Tahiri cried. "Wild banthas couldn't stop us!"

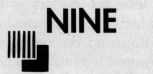 NINE

Tahiri leaned forward and took one of the trico filters that lay on Sannah's lap. Anakin stared in surprise at his friend. "I haven't forgotten that I can't swim," Tahiri explained. "But there's no way I'm going to miss this. Anyway, as long as I can breathe underwater, it doesn't matter that I can't swim. You and Lyric can help me."

Tahiri took out her multitool and cut down the filter Sannah had handed her until it was the right size for her small face. Then she let Sannah tie the algae-filled filter over her nose and mouth. For a moment, Tahiri couldn't breathe and a feeling of dizzying panic clutched at her throat. She forced herself to relax, just as she'd seen Anakin do. When she could finally breathe, she moved to the edge of the crystal blue waters.

Sannah handed Tahiri and Anakin several

large rocks to place in their pockets before they entered the water. "You will need the added weight," Sannah explained. "You are going deep."

"I'll help you," Lyric sang up to Tahiri, and beckoned her friend into the waters with her pale, graceful arms. Tahiri dipped her toe into the warm water. She sat down on the rocky edge of the pool and slowly lowered herself until the water swallowed her body. Lyric floated by Tahiri's side, her arm around the girl's waist, her powerful tail fin keeping Tahiri's head above water. Anakin slipped into the water and moved to Tahiri's other side. He, too, wrapped an arm around her waist.

"Ready?" Anakin said to Tahiri.

"As I'll ever be," Tahiri replied with a nervous smile.

"Do not be frightened," Lyric called to Tahiri. "We will be traveling deep within the waters to the place where the oldest of my species live. There, I hope, you will find the answer to your questions."

Tahiri allowed herself to sink below the surface of the crystal blue water. Anakin and Lyric kept hold of her as they descended into the depths. At first Tahiri felt panicky and breathed through the filter in ragged gasps. Her eyes rolled wildly from side to side. Once, she tried to struggle out of the arms of her friends, but they held her steady until she relaxed. Tahiri saw hundreds of elder Melodies swimming around them as Lyric pulled her friends deeper and deeper with swift, powerful thrusts of her tail fin. The elders were so beautiful and graceful, Tahiri thought as they traveled through the crystal waters.

Strange, Tahiri pondered, as she studied the underwater world, it was light beneath the surface of the water. She had expected to be swallowed in blackness. The purple rocks of the mountain actually glowed, and streaks of neon scribbled through the waters as Anakin and Lyric dragged her downward.

"Kick with your feet," a soft gurgling voice said from behind Tahiri.

Tahiri turned her head and saw an elder, his blond hair, as long as her own, floating in tendrils around his face. His tail was a darker shade of pink than Lyric's, and it sparkled in the waters. "Kick with your feet," the elder said again. Tahiri began to kick. "Let her go for a moment," the Melodie instructed Lyric and Anakin. Slowly they unwound their arms from Tahiri's waist. "Use your arms like this," the Melodie said as he demonstrated how to move through the waters by pulling his arms from his head to his side. Tahiri tried. And, although she didn't shoot through the water as he did, she did move, all by herself.

"Am I swimming?" Tahiri gurgled from beneath her mask.

"Yes," the Melodie said with a large smile and a laugh that sounded like a waterfall.

"This is my father," Lyric sang out to Tahiri and Anakin. "His name is Gyle." Lyric floated over to the elder, and he wrapped her in an embrace.

"You have helped bring me my daughter. Thank you," Gyle said. Just then a school of silver-backed fish streamed through the Jedi candidates. Tahiri panicked, and tried to thrash her way back to the surface. Several of the elders encircled her and swam her back down to Anakin and Lyric. "There is nothing to fear down here, little one," Gyle said when Tahiri was back in their midst. "Come, there is not much time, we must go farther. Tahiri, hold my hand. Anakin, hold Lyric's."

Gyle and Lyric led the Jedi candidates swiftly through their world. Tahiri and Anakin took in its beauty as they streamed through the waters. There were glowing caverns, vibrant-colored fish striped with shades of blues, greens, and yellows, and elders everywhere, playing in the liquid of their world. Gyle came to a stop before the mouth of a purple cavern whose surface was lined with stones that glistened red. "Aragon!" Gyle called into the cave.

There was a rush of water, and then the elder floated gently out. He was smaller than Gyle, and his long hair flowed in a cloud of white around his face. His yellow eyes were large as he studied Anakin and Tahiri, who floated in front of him in their orange academy jumpsuits.

"Aragon, these children are Jedi candidates from the academy we sent Lyric to on Yavin 4," Gyle began. "They have come to ask about the strange symbols that are carved in some of the tunnels and on the rock wall of an avril's lair. Since you're the keeper of legends, and the oldest of us, I thought you might know of these things."

"I think I have seen the symbols you speak of," Aragon gurgled. "But I can no longer remember where, or what they mean. Ask something else of me—I can tell you legends about almost anything beneath these waters, but the old story you ask about was told to me more than a hundred years ago. It is a mere whisper in my ancient mind."

Anakin and Tahiri couldn't hide the disappointment in their eyes.

"I am sorry," Aragon said sadly. "I see that I have failed you."

Tahiri let Aragon's words sink in. Aragon hadn't failed them, she thought. It was she and Anakin who had failed, who had been unable to discover a way to decipher the strange symbols. And in failing, they had given up any chance to destroy the evil that held children trapped within the golden globe. Tahiri thought about the Jedi Code. Luke Skywalker had said that there was no try, only do. But she and Anakin had tried. Or had they?

"Anakin, Aragon once knew the information we need," Tahiri thought out loud. "So the memory is somewhere in his mind, he just can't find it, right?"

Anakin nodded. He saw at once what Tahiri meant.

"Aragon," he said, "would you let us try to help you remember where the symbols are and what they mean?"

The elder met the boy's ice blue gaze. It was clear to him that the children's request was not one of idle curiosity; they truly needed to know. "Yes," he replied gravely. "Help me to remember if you can."

TEN

Anakin floated before the elder named Aragon as he struggled to put into words a skill he'd always had. He could remember when he was two years old and took apart his first droid with his siblings, Jaina and Jacen. He could remember the first time he'd seen a lightsaber, heard about the Force, learned about good and evil. But how did he travel through his mind, picking up memories as easily as he'd drawn the symbols carved in the Palace of the Woolamander?

"Close your eyes," Anakin said to Aragon. "Think back to the one who told you the stories. To the one who was the keeper of legends before you."

"That was my mother," Aragon gurgled softly. "Her name was Esla. She was taught the legends from her father, and so on and so on, stretching back thousands of years."

"Can you see her in your mind's eye?" Anakin asked softly.

"She was beautiful," Aragon replied. "Thick, long, black hair that reached well past her waist, lovely yellow eyes, lips the color of the palest pink webbing. She told me the stories every day of my life, until she passed away. We'd swim together in the waters and her pure voice would ring with legends . . . the legends of my people, and of the ones who came to ask our help."

"Who were they?" Anakin asked, trying to control the tension in his voice. Trying to gently lead the elder down the path to remembrance.

"I cannot recall their names," Aragon said thickly as he struggled through the dust-covered corridors of his memory. "Only that they came to Sistra in search of help for their children. Children who were enslaved by some unnamed darkness. Our own children found them wandering through the mountains and brought them to the elders. But we couldn't help them!" Aragon cried, remembering his mother's grief in the telling of the legend. "We could not leave our moon, the water. And so they left their messages carved in the rocks and tunnels of our world, in the hopes that someday someone might read them and come to their aid."

"And the symbols?" Anakin asked. "Do you know what each one means?"

"I'm afraid I do not," Aragon answered. "I saw some once, deep in the belly of the mountain where the purella dwell, and my mother told me what they meant. But it was so long ago, so long ago . . ." Aragon fell silent, lost in his memories.

Another dead end, Anakin thought wearily. He felt his breathing becoming more labored, and knew it was time to resurface. "Thank you," he said to Aragon. "The algae in our filters won't last much longer," he told Lyric. "We need to go back to the surface."

Lyric looked sadly at her two friends. "I'm sorry," she said as she and Gyle propelled Anakin and Tahiri away from the elder.

"Wait," Tahiri cried. She broke away from Gyle and clumsily kicked her way back to the elder.

"What is it, child?" Aragon asked.

"You said that you couldn't remember what each symbol meant," Tahiri said breathlessly, her head pounding as the oxygen from the algae grew thinner, "but do you remember what the message was? Because if you do, we can find it in the bottom of the mountain, decipher what each symbol means from the whole message, and then use them to translate the carvings on our own moon!"

Aragon was quiet for a moment. He closed his eyes and dove into the dark recesses of his mind, searching for the information Tahiri asked. "I saw the strange symbols at the base of the deepest tunnel of Sistra," Aragon said slowly, wrenching the long-forgotten memory from a corner in his mind. "My mother told me the symbols read, 'Peace to all. We are the Massassi. We beg the ones who read this message to travel to the fourth moon. Break the curse that the evil Jedi Knight Exar Kun made to enslave the Massassi and imprison our children. We cannot break the curse ourselves, but will leave a message in our palace to help those who can.' "

Aragon met Tahiri's green eyes with his own. "Does that help you, child?" he asked.

"Yes," Tahiri gasped. "Thank you." Gyle and Lyric grasped the hands of the Jedi candidates and quickly led them back to the surface, their tail fins furiously swishing through the crystal waters, scribbling streaks of neon behind them. Tahiri felt her lungs tightening as she ran out of oxygen. She clawed at her pockets and released the rocks that weighted her down. The pounding in her head became dizzying, and she was afraid that she might lose consciousness. Just in time, she and Anakin burst through the surface. They ripped off their filters and greedily gulped in air.

Lyric helped Tahiri swim to the side of the waters, and several Melodie children pulled her out onto the rocks, where Anakin already sat.

"We've got to find those carvings," Anakin said weakly to Tahiri. "Sannah," he said to the girl beside him, "can you take us to the deepest tunnel in the mountain?"

"That is where the purella live," Sannah said in a voice laced with fear. "They are enormous red-bristled spiders with glowing orange eyes. It is strange that you have not seen a purella—every year one comes to the cove to snatch a child or a changeling. We were lucky this time. The purella is a vicious beast who drags away her prey and traps it within the web of her lair. There is no escape from the web. The victim is consumed slowly," Sannah explained in a hollow voice.

"Will you take us there?" Anakin asked again.

"I will lead you to the beginning of the deepest tunnel," Sannah finally replied. "But I will not journey to its base. To do so means certain death. I am willing to risk my life for both of you," Sannah said, looking from Anakin to Tahiri. "But facing the purella is not risking life, it is embracing death."

Anakin and Tahiri rose to their feet and walked to the water's edge. It was time to say good-bye to Lyric. They were determined to unravel the riddle that had held the Massassi children prisoner for thousands of years.

"You are leaving now," Lyric said sadly as she floated on the surface of the water. "I know that you must return to the academy, but I don't want you to leave."

"Lyric, we'll miss you," Tahiri said softly.

"You are the two best friends I've ever had," Lyric said in a voice like dropping tears. "I won't forget you, and I'll help to teach the Melodie children all that I learned at the academy. Perhaps someday you'll come back to visit me?"

"I hope so," Anakin said. He didn't mention that there was a chance he and Tahiri might never leave Lyric's mountain. A chance that they would be devoured by an enormous, red-bristled spider. "Good-bye, Lyric. May the Force be with you," Anakin said.

"And both of you," Lyric replied. Large salty tears dropped from her eyes and plinked sadly down. Then she dove beneath the surface of the crystal blue waters. The last Anakin and Tahiri saw of their friend was a flash of her glistening pink tail fin.

⫿⫾ ELEVEN

She was beside herself with hunger and rage.
Her underbelly yawned and screamed for the
sweet taste of a Melodie. She'd been so close.
They hadn't even seen her clinging to the top of
the rocks overhead as they'd raced through the
passageway with the changelings toward the
crystal waters. She'd been ready to drop, to gouge
the sharp pincers that lined her mouth into
tender flesh. Then she would have flushed her
prey with enough poison to immobilize, but not to
kill. She liked her food alive.

The agonizing scream of a raith as one of the
Melodies ran the creature through with a spear
broke her pleasant anticipation. She crept along
the passageway to drink in the scene with glowing eyes. She'd never seen a Melodie kill so easily.
And she'd experienced something she'd never felt

before. Fear. She didn't like it. Didn't like it at all. Her pincers clicked frantically as she remembered how she'd skittered back through the passageways, away from her prey, to the safety of the tunnel where she dwelled.

The purella picked her way across her thick black web. The web she'd spun to ensnare a Melodie. Caught in its center was a small raith. She'd come across the black rodent in one of the middle tunnels, and dropped on it in hunger and frustration. Her pincers had plunged deep into the tender skin of its neck, filling the raith with enough venom to paralyze it so she could drag it back to her web by its thick green tail.

When the venom had worn off, the raith had struggled in the thick stickiness of the purella's web. But the more it had writhed, the more the web had bound its body. Now it could only move its hard, black eyes. They rolled from side to side. She could taste the raith's terror, just as she would soon taste its meat.

The purella slowly moved toward the rodent, her eight legs picking through the web with care. She, too, could be caught if she allowed her bristly backside to touch its gummy strands. But that never happened. She moved with an eerie grace, never losing her balance. There was no need to rush once her prey was ensnared. There was no escape from a purella's web.

She felt a slight tremor in the web, and fixed her eyes on the raith. He hadn't moved. Couldn't move. Another tremor, dancing along the strand on tiptoes. The purella skittered back to the edge of her web. A web that not only trapped her prey, but served as a perfectly tuned alarm system that picked up every movement and vibration. Something was traveling in the lower tunnel.

The purella usually had to hunt for her prey in the mid-passages of Sistra, but once in a while a raith or reel would come down to the lower tunnel. When that happened, she was always ready. Orange eyes narrowed as she glanced at the ensnared raith. Her belly ached, but it would have to wait. When she returned, she hoped, she'd have more food. That would be good, because she was hungry. Very hungry.

She slid her body through the crevice that led to her den. Hopping to the rocks, she began to move up the tunnel. A small stone was dislodged from above, and nervously she sprang onto the side wall of the passageway. She flattened her body against the rocks, a two-meter blot of red against the dark purple of the stones. Any creature looking would see her, but in her experience, her prey didn't pay attention to what they couldn't hear. At least the reels and raiths didn't. The Melodies were different, more difficult to trick and snare. Catching them as regular food was too much work—which was why she waited for the changing time. She didn't like to work too hard for her food. And there was no need to.

When she heard the sounds she was momentarily puzzled. They were neither the snarls and grunts of raiths nor the slithering hisses of reels. And then she felt the familiar pains in her underbelly, felt thick ropes of saliva begin to form in her mouth and drip heavily from her pincers. Melodies. Never before had they come here. They knew this was the dwelling place of the purella.

She did not pause to wonder why they were here. Instead she skittered to the top of the passageway, over the strange carvings that marred the purple rocks. She would wait, unseen, above them. And when the Melodies came through the tunnel, came to her, she would be ready. Oh yes, she thought greedily, she would be ready.

TWELVE

"This is as far as I can take you," Sannah whispered. She stood in the rippling pool of yellow that blazed from the torch she carried. Deep within the mountain, there were no holes or cracks in the rocks to let in the soft evening light. As Sannah, Anakin, and Tahiri had descended into the bowels of Sistra, they had been swallowed by the darkness. Without Sannah's torches, they would not have been able to see.

"What you are about to do is folly," Sannah warned for the last time. She'd spent the past hour trying to turn the Jedi candidates back from what, to her, meant certain death. But her words had fallen on deaf ears, and there was nothing left to say. "May your Force be with you," she solemnly whispered to Anakin and Tahiri. And then she turned and became a receding circle of yellow light, consumed moments later by darkness.

Anakin held his torch high to dispel the blackness of the passageway before him. He heard Aragon's translation of the carved symbols ringing in his ears. If he and Tahiri could see the carvings that Aragon had remembered in this tunnel, and then use Aragon's translation to decipher the symbols, they'd be able to do the same with the ones from the Palace of the Woolamander.

"Anakin, we forgot to bring something to copy down the symbols," Tahiri whispered, interrupting her friend's thoughts.

"I'll remember them," Anakin reassured Tahiri. Just as he'd recalled the symbols from the palace, he knew he'd be able to draw the carvings in this passageway once they were safely back on Yavin 4. Anakin turned to Tahiri, whose green eyes glowed nervously in the pale yellow light of their torch. "Are you ready?" Anakin asked.

"Let's get this over with," Tahiri agreed. "I can sense danger."

"Me too," Anakin said softly. "Me too." Slowly he led Tahiri into the passageway. He held his torch high, his eyes darting from side to side, searching for the red spider he'd never seen but knew enough to be afraid of. The passageway dove steeply into the mountain, and several times Anakin and Tahiri almost lost their footing.

"Anakin, over there!" Tahiri cried. She pointed to a smooth segment in the rocks. Then she raced ahead until she stood before the same strangely twined symbols they'd seen in the palace on Yavin 4. Her eyes raced across the message left in the walls of Sistra by the ancient Massassi. "This is it, Anakin!" she called back happily.

Anakin walked carefully toward his friend. He sensed danger, grave danger. His ice blue eyes studied the rocks around him, but he saw nothing, heard nothing. Maybe all the stories he'd heard from Sannah about the purella had been exaggerations. And perhaps the warnings that were screaming inside his head were his own imagination. Still, all his senses jangled with alarm. "Tahiri," Anakin began. But it was too late.

The purella that had been silently waiting above the carvings dropped on top of Tahiri, flattening her with its giant red-bristled body. In a split second, eight legs wrapped around Tahiri and four large pincers sank through her orange academy jumpsuit. Tahiri screamed, but her cries ceased as her body jerked once, then fell limp in the spider's deadly embrace.

Anakin watched in horror as the purella turned from Tahiri and slowly approached him, its double-jointed legs moving with casual grace. He began to back away, his torch held in front of his body to ward off the spider's attack. The creature's eyes glowed orange as they studied him carefully. Anakin's glance flew around the tunnel. It was roughly two meters wide, and so was the spider. There was nowhere to dodge or roll from the creature's attack. So Anakin stood his ground, and when the spider moved forward, he lashed out with his torch, searing one of its legs. Thick ropes of yellow spittle flew from the spider's jaws as it recoiled in pain.

The purella's savage eyes glowered at Anakin. And then she sprang toward him, crashing the torch from his grip and quenching its flame. The giant red spider knocked Anakin flat on his back, pinning his arms and legs with four of her eight limbs. He stared up into the spider's horrid face, all jaws, pincers, and glowing eyes that lit the tunnel in orange flame. Anakin tried to struggle, but the spider was too heavy. The creature studied him as he fought, then languidly sank her needle-sharp pincers into his body. Anakin felt pain, and then the venom coursed through his veins, numbing and paralyzing him.

At least he was still awake, Anakin thought. So was Tahiri. The purella pulled both the Jedi candidates along the rocky passageway, their bodies limp with poison, but their minds racing to figure out a way to save themselves. Anakin's eyes rolled from side to side—they were all he could move. He saw Tahiri looking over at him, her large green eyes wide with fear. The purella continued to drag them deeper into the mountain. Then, quite suddenly, the creature stopped.

Anakin lay in the tunnel, unable to move, as he watched the spider wrap Tahiri in its supple red legs and carry her through a crevice in the rocks. Minutes later, the awful creature returned and dragged him through the same crack. Anakin was carried across a thick black web and deposited next to Tahiri and a small raith. The raith was still alive, but hopelessly entangled in the thick black web of the purella. Through the only light in the cave—a surprisingly bright, eerie orange glow that came from the purella's eyes—Anakin saw that the raith had stopped struggling. He also saw that the more the rodent had struggled, the tighter he'd been bound in the spider's web. Anakin wanted to tell Tahiri that when the venom wore off, she shouldn't struggle. But at the moment he couldn't move his mouth. He grimly hoped the venom would wear off before the spider decided it was dinnertime.

The purella moved away from her prey to the far side of the web. She would wait for the venom to wear off the Melodies. Then they would try to escape, as her prey always did, and the sticky strands of her web would bind them. Once they could no longer move, she'd have all the time she

83

wanted to savor their warm flesh. She studied her burned leg and the scorched part of her underbelly. She hated when they fought her, like the one had done with the fire. He had hurt her, and she didn't like to be hurt. But in the end, that one would suffer much more than she had. Oh yes, she thought to herself, he would suffer.

THIRTEEN

Anakin felt sensation returning to his fingers and toes. Feeling slowly crept up his legs in sharp pricks, swirled across his rib cage, prickled in a stream of warm pain the length of his shoulder blades and neck, and eventually danced all the way to his scalp. But he lay still. "Tahiri," Anakin said breathlessly, "don't move."

Tahiri nodded, but didn't reply. She'd also seen the raith, and knew that her struggles would only entangle her further in the sticky threads that glued her body to the web, except for one arm that had fallen limply across her belly. Part of one of Anakin's legs had fallen bent at the knee, but otherwise he too was completely trapped in the purella's deadly snare.

Anakin had an idea. If he and Tahiri were glued to the sticky black threads, why couldn't

85

the spider be caught in her own web? He'd watched the purella navigate through the web, careful not to touch any of its threads with her bristles. What if he and Tahiri could make the creature lose her balance, topple into her own trap? He looked over at the purella, folded in the corner of the web. Her glowing orange eyes were fixed on them. If only they could topple the immense spider onto her back, where thick red bristles rose.

"Tahiri, can you rock the web without getting yourself stuck any more than you already are?" Anakin breathed out of the side of his mouth.

"What do you have in mind?" Tahiri murmured back.

"We've got to try to trap that thing in its own web," Anakin said softly. Tahiri turned her head minutely and met Anakin's ice blue eyes with determined green ones.

Slowly, Tahiri raised her right arm and began to pump it up and down. The purella watched her movements, but didn't rise. Tahiri pumped harder, and the web began to shake. At the same time, Anakin pushed with his left foot, the joint of his free knee hitching up and down. They worked together, and the web began to rock. As it moved, the Jedi candidates pumped their free limbs harder, bouncing the web up and down.

The purella rose. Her prey was beginning to

struggle, to bind themselves in her snare. The quivers in the lines drew her toward them, as a spider is always drawn to the tremors of prey in her web. She moved slowly, keeping her delicate balance within the strands of her web.

"She's coming!" Tahiri cried.

"Keep bouncing the web," Anakin replied. He pounded his foot against the strands. The web was now steadily rocking. The purella paused, unaccustomed to so much motion within her web, to struggles of prey that lasted so long. Her body rose and fell as Anakin and Tahiri pressured the web into waves. Then the spider began to move forward again, the hairless base of her legs dancing through the gummy strands until she stopped, less than a half meter from her prey.

"Anakin, it's not working!" Tahiri cried in terror. The purella fixed her with gleaming orange eyes. It was poised to attack once again, jaws open wide, thick yellow saliva dripping in anticipation.

Anakin stared beyond the creature, up into the recesses of the den. The rock above him was at least eight meters away. "Use the Force to lift the web!" Anakin cried to Tahiri. He closed his eyes and focused on the energy field generated by all living things. Focused on the web, the air, the form of the purella, and his own body. In his mind he was one with the energy field, using it to cause the web to rise like an immense tidal wave. Anakin felt himself lifting, so high he imagined his body might smash into the rocks far above the web. "Drop, now!" Anakin yelled to his friend. He pushed with his mind, and felt his body plummeting down, down, down, until he thought he might be swallowed up in the belly of the mountain.

Anakin's eyes flew open. He felt the web rising again from his and Tahiri's efforts, falling and rising, and falling again. It was rebounding so quickly that his stomach rolled with nausea and his vision came in sharp flashes.

"Anakin, I think we did it!" Tahiri cried into the whirlwind.

Anakin tore his eyes from the rocks above, which ebbed and flowed before his vision. A searing stab of fear shot through his belly. Where was the spider? Had she leapt safely from the web? Was she now calmly waiting on the walls of the den for the strands to stop rising? Then he saw her. The motion of the web had thrown the spider into the center of her own deadly snare. She'd landed on the bristles of her back, her red underbelly exposed to the air. The creature writhed and twisted, trying to escape from the gumminess of her threads. As she struggled, the web wrapped around her spastic legs, tightening until their only movement came in twitches. Anakin could see one of the spider's glowing orange eyes, and he didn't have to use the Force to sense the creature's rage.

The web slowly came to rest, stuck to the lower rocks. "We need to figure out a way to unstick ourselves," Anakin said to Tahiri. Although they hadn't become further ensnared in the web as it had rocked, both of them were still firmly glued down. "Any ideas, Tahiri?" Anakin asked.

"How about this?" Tahiri said with a grin as she reached into her jumpsuit and pulled out her multitool. With a click, she snapped out the knife she'd used to cut down her trico filter. Using her free arm, she carefully began to cut around her body, and when she was free enough, she leaned over and began to cut through the thick strands around Anakin. Then she handed the blade to her friend so that he could cut around his other side, then lean back to cut the places around her body that she couldn't reach without risking sticking herself on the web.

It was slow, tricky work, but a half hour later, Anakin cut the last thread that held them in the web. They dangled for a split second, then dropped the short distance to the rocks below. Anakin looked up at the purella. Her orange eyes glowered in rage, but she didn't move. The spider was completely stuck in her own web. "Let's get out of here, Tahiri," Anakin said softly.

The Jedi candidates climbed up the rocks and

through the narrow crevice that the purella had carried them through earlier. As they left the spider's dwelling, they were swallowed up by the darkness of the passageway. Tahiri reached through the gloom to find Anakin's hand.

"Don't worry," Anakin said in the darkness, "I remember the way out." He gave Tahiri's hand a squeeze, then led her through the steep tunnel. They walked softly, both worried that another purella might find them. But they managed to reach the top of the lower tunnel without encountering an orange-eyed predator.

Still, they weren't prepared for what awaited them as they rounded the corner.

FOURTEEN

Tahiri screamed as her body brushed against the thing at the top of the tunnel. It was warm, and alive, and she felt frustration and fear rise in her belly. Enough was enough; she was too tired and sore to defend herself against another attack.

"Don't strike," a soft voice cried. It was Sannah. She had returned to the lower tunnel. Sannah lit her trico torch, and Anakin and Tahiri saw the Melodie in its golden light. Her yellow eyes were large and scared. "I couldn't leave," she began, nervously twisting her straight brown hair around pale fingers. "I had to know that you were all right."

"Let's get out of here," Anakin said urgently.

Sannah nodded, then began to lead the Jedi candidates back to the middle passage of the mountain. She stopped once, frozen as she listened to the soft scratching of raith claws overhead. But the creatures didn't sense the three children, and after the rodents had passed Sannah moved forward. Soon they reached the middle passageway, where morning light lazily drifted through cracks and holes in the mountain. Here the tunnel divided in two directions. One went back to Lyric's world, the other led up to the portal of Sistra and the brown green tundra of the moon.

"We know the way from here," Anakin said softly. "Will you be safe? Or do you want us to take you back to your people before we leave?" Anakin asked.

"No," Sannah replied.

"No you won't be safe, or no you don't want us to go back with you?" Tahiri asked the girl.

"No, I don't want to go back to my world," Sannah said in a quavering voice, her yellow eyes fixed on the two Jedi candidates.

"What do you mean?" Anakin asked.

"I want to go with you," Sannah replied evenly. "I want to study at the Jedi academy, learn about the Force, and develop the skills I need to help protect my people."

"We can't take you with us," Anakin gently explained. "We're not Jedi Knights; we don't have the authority to bring anyone to the academy.

Only Luke Skywalker and the other Jedi can do that."

"Why?" Sannah said.

"Yes, why?" Tahiri echoed, as she mulled over the idea.

"Tahiri," Anakin said in exasperation, "you know we can't just bring Sannah back to Yavin 4!"

"But you saw the way she fought the raith," Tahiri replied. "She's sensitive to the Force—I can feel it, Anakin!"

"You've seen what the predators on this planet do to my people," Sannah said as she met Anakin's ice blue eyes. "The children are defenseless. For every avril we successfully fight off, there is another that steals two of us away. For every raith we spear, five more devour our eggs. And judging from the time it took you to leave the lower passage, and the tears in your jumpsuit, you've seen the strength of the purella. We cannot fight them at all!" Sannah cried.

"It is not in anger that I ask you to take me," Sannah said, steadying her voice. "Though controlling my fury is something I will have to learn. Take me because I feel the thing you call the Force. Take me because I will pledge myself to the peace and knowledge of the Jedi, and to the use of the Force not in anger, but only in defense."

93

"Do the elders know that you want to leave with us and attend the academy?" Tahiri asked. They couldn't take the girl with them without the elder Melodies's permission.

"Yes," Sannah replied. "I leave with their blessing. Especially Lyric's."

"If Luke Skywalker doesn't feel you are strong in the Force, you'll probably be returned to Yavin 8," Anakin said slowly.

"I'll take that risk," Sannah replied. "I'm only nine years old. If I am permitted to stay until my changing ceremony, I'll return with the skills to help. And regardless of Luke Skywalker's decision, at least I will have tried to help my people."

Anakin turned toward the portal. "Come on, then," he called over his shoulder to Sannah. Tahiri grinned at the girl and grabbed her hand. The three children emerged from Sistra into the early-morning sunlight. They paused on the purple rocks and breathed in the fresh air of hope.

Tahiri, Anakin, and Sannah climbed down Sistra quickly. Anakin hoped that Old Peckhum had returned with the supply ship; he and Tahiri were too tired for another battle. Moments later, his hopes were answered as the longhaired old courier raced toward the children.

"I've been searching all night for you!" Peckhum cried, his hands wrapped around an old-fashioned blaster rifle. "I couldn't find the

portal to Lyric's world in the mountains. Where
have you been—I was so worried!" He didn't
pause to wait for an answer. "You look terrible,"
he said as he studied Tahiri's and Anakin's torn,
dirt-covered clothing. "Are you all right? And
who's this?" He gestured toward Sannah.

"We're fine," Anakin assured the frantic pilot.

"This is Sannah," Tahiri added. "She's coming
back to Yavin 4 with us."

Peckhum was too relieved to argue with them.
All he wanted to do was get safely back to the
Jedi academy. No more baby-sitting for him!

The children and the courier began walking
toward the shuttle. They did not encounter any
raiths or reels as they traveled. And, when they
heard the distant shriek of an avril as they
boarded, Anakin smiled at its fierce, though
strangely beautiful, cry.

FIFTEEN

Sannah had never been on a shuttle. She sat next to Peckhum and stared out the window as her world shrank from view and the shuttle was engulfed by the evening skies. Anakin could hear her questions drift back from the front of the craft, and visions of Lyric, who had been in the same seat only yesterday, swam through his mind. He wondered if he'd ever see her red ringlets, glistening pink tail fin, and gentle yellow eyes again. He hoped Lyric would be happy in the crystal waters of her world. And what about Sannah? Anakin hoped that Uncle Luke would allow the girl to study at the academy. The young Melodie was sensitive to the Force. He had felt the strength in her, and so had Tahiri.

"Do you think Master Luke will be angry at us

for bringing her?" Tahiri asked with a nervous nod toward Sannah.

"I'm not sure," Anakin replied. He, too, felt his stomach tying itself in knots. They made a brief stop to deliver Peckhum's supplies to another cargo ship that circled Yavin, waiting for the *Lightning Rod*. Then, the pilot headed their shuttle back to Yavin 4.

It was all Anakin could do to make himself stand up and move toward the door when the ship had landed. A jolt of terror ran through him. If Sannah told Uncle Luke about the carvings he and Tahiri had risked their lives to find in the lower tunnel of Sistra, his uncle would want to know why. And there was no way he could lie to Luke Skywalker. Anakin would be forced to tell him about the messages the Massassi had left, and the golden globe in the Palace of the Woola-mander. If that happened, the prophesy that the Jedi Master Ikrit had foretold would occur: the globe would shatter into a thousand pieces of crystal and the children trapped within its glittering sands would be lost.

"Sannah," Anakin called urgently. The Melodie walked back to him and Tahiri. "I need to ask you a favor."

"Anything," Sannah instantly replied.

Anakin steadied his voice. "Sannah, I need you to promise not to mention the strange carvings in the rocks of Sistra to Luke Skywalker," Anakin said. "Please don't tell him that Tahiri and I risked our lives to read the carvings in the lower tunnel. If you do, countless beings will be in grave danger."

"I would never want to get you into any trouble," Sannah said softly. "I promise."

"Thank you, Sannah," Anakin said with relief. "Now please wait inside the shuttle until we tell Uncle Luke that we brought you." Anakin didn't want to spring Sannah on his uncle without an explanation.

Sannah nodded and shrank back from the shuttle door as it hissed open.

As he watched the door open, Luke Skywalker was not pleased. He was dismayed to see his nephew and Tahiri emerge bruised and battered. Both students were covered with streaks of purple dirt, and their orange academy jumpsuits were torn. In addition, thick strands of what looked like spider webbing hung from the leg of Anakin's jumpsuit, and blue-green algae was dried to the tops of Tahiri's bare feet.

"Hi, Uncle Luke," Anakin said with a little smile.

"Welcome home," Luke Skywalker said in a voice ringing with concern. "You are both a mess. What happened to you on Yavin 8?"

"We ran into some pretty nasty creatures,"

Tahiri said with a nervous grin. "But Lyric's changing was a success."

"I want both of you to see the medical droid about your wounds," Luke Skywalker solemnly instructed as he wrapped his arms around Anakin's and Tahiri's shoulders and drew them away from the shuttle. "We'll discuss your adventures after I'm sure you're all right. And I may have a word with Peckhum."

"Er, Uncle Luke, there's something we need to talk about before we go to see the medical droid," Anakin said nervously.

Luke Skywalker turned to face his nephew. "Can't it wait?" he inquired.

"Well, it's not exactly an it," Anakin began. "It's a she. Her name is Sannah. She's a Melodie we met on Yavin 8. . . . I think she's sensitive to the Force," Anakin continued weakly, embarrassed to even suggest to his uncle that he thought he could recognize strength in the Force when he was only a Jedi candidate.

"Tell me about her," Luke Skywalker said.

"She fought a raith," Tahiri began. "That's a giant black, hairy rodent with jagged teeth. She did it using the Force—I know she did because I felt it. She wants to study at the academy so she can learn to protect the Melodie children from the predators on her moon," Tahiri went on without taking a breath. "There's so many of them—

avrils, raiths, and reels, and enormous red-bristled spiders named purellas which, believe me, are vicious." Then Tahiri, too, faltered before Luke's silence and the calm of his pale blue eyes. "She's in the shuttle," she finally murmured.

Sannah appeared in the doorway of the shiny craft, then slowly came down the ramp. The rustling of her light green tunic was the only sound that broke the silence of Luke Skywalker's stare. She approached the Jedi Master, her large yellow eyes never leaving his face.

"Welcome to the Jedi academy, Sannah," Luke said when the young Melodie reached him. "We have a lot to discuss. Anakin, Tahiri, please go see the medic. I'll take care of your friend," Luke instructed.

Tahiri and Anakin didn't want to leave Sannah. But there was no disobeying the stern note in Luke's voice. They both turned and left the hangar.

"Do you think Master Luke will let her stay?" Tahiri whispered as they headed to the turbolift that would take them to the upper levels of the Great Temple.

"I hope so, Tahiri," Anakin replied. "But I just don't know."

SIXTEEN

Anakin and Tahiri hunched over several sheets of paper on the stone floor of Anakin's room. They'd returned from the academy medical droid only a short while before. She'd cleaned their cuts and bandaged Tahiri's ribs. Tahiri had been right: the reel that had tried to crush her had cracked one of them. The medical droid had also taken a sample of their blood to make sure the purella's venom had left their systems. It had. And, except for the cuts and a few bruises, she said the two Jedi candidates were fine.

It was late afternoon, and after a shower and a change of clothing Tahiri had gone to Anakin's room. Now both candidates sat hard at work, trying to decipher the symbols left by the Massassi.

"Anakin, are you done writing down the message from the lower tunnel of Sistra?" Tahiri asked impatiently.

"Almost," Anakin said, his eyes closed as he recalled the carvings and scribbled them down.

Tahiri studied the symbols from the Palace of the Woolamander. She desperately hoped that they'd be able to decipher them from the translation Aragon had recalled of the carvings on Yavin 8. To do so would mean breaking down the carvings from the lower tunnel of Sistra and matching each symbol to the words Aragon had remembered. Tahiri fervently hoped that the elder Melodie's memory hadn't been faulty. If it had, they wouldn't be able to translate the carvings in the palace. And they would not be able to help the children trapped within the golden globe.

Tahiri looked at another sheet of paper. On it were the words Aragon had spoken. Words that Anakin had written down moments ago, as if Aragon's voice still echoed in his head. "Peace to all. We are the Massassi. We beg the ones who read this message to travel to the fourth moon. Break the curse that the evil Jedi Knight Exar Kun made to enslave the Massassi and imprison our children. We cannot break the curse ourselves, but will leave a message in our palace to help those who can." Tahiri had just finished reading when there was a soft knock on Anakin's door.

"Just a minute," Anakin called as he scrambled to hide the sheets of paper he and Tahiri were working on. "Come," he called.

The door opened and Luke Skywalker stood looking at the two candidates. "The medical droid told me that your wounds have been treated," Master Luke said as he moved to sit on a stone chair. "Anakin, it is lucky that you weren't badly hurt, or your mother would have had my head," Luke said sternly. "I'm very glad that you both are safe and back at the academy."

Anakin heard the note of concern in his uncle's voice. Leia Organa Solo was Uncle Luke's sister, and his mother had entrusted her youngest son to Luke Skywalker's care. There was no way Uncle Luke would accept any unnecessary actions on his or Tahiri's part that would have put them in danger. If he learned that either had been foolhardy on Yavin 8, Luke Skywalker would not only be displeased, but they might be sent home. Anakin desperately hoped that Sannah hadn't mentioned the carvings.

"I've heard from Sannah that you fought bravely to protect the Melodies from predators," Luke Skywalker continued. "That you used the Force to protect your friend, her people, and yourselves."

Luke Skywalker studied Anakin's young face. He hoped his nephew understood the gravity of the situation he'd survived. "I'm pleased that Lyric survived the changing and is now an elder," Master Luke continued. "However, we must discuss Sannah."

Anakin's heart sank. Sannah was being sent home. "We're sorry, Uncle Luke," he began. "It's just that we couldn't deny her the chance to help her people—"

"Don't apologize," Luke Skywalker interrupted. "It's true that the Melodies on Yavin 8 are unable to protect themselves well from the predators that roam their moon. That's one of the reasons that Tionne brought Lyric to the academy. Even though Lyric was close to the time of changing, Tionne recognized that she was strong in the Force. We both hoped to teach Lyric enough so that she could return to her moon and help the Melodies. And I think we were successful. Lyric will begin to seek those of her people who are sensitive to the Force, and to help them understand the Force. She herself understands it deeply, even though her time here was short. Sannah's time with us will be longer."

"Did you just say what I think you said?" Tahiri cried.

Before Luke Skywalker could answer, Sannah appeared in the doorway in an orange academy jumpsuit. Tahiri leapt toward her new friend and enfolded her in a hug.

"You were right—she is strong in the Force," Luke Skywalker said. He embraced the three Jedi candidates before he strode from the room and left them alone.

Anakin turned toward Sannah. "Welcome to the academy," he said softly.

"Thank you," Sannah replied with an enormous smile. "Thank you for bringing me here. I've got to go see the Jedi Knight Tionne now," she explained. "She's going to show me where my room is and tell me more about the academy." Sannah turned to leave Anakin's room. "By the way," she said over her shoulder. "I didn't mention the carvings in the lower tunnel to Master Luke. Your secret is safe with me."

Anakin and Tahiri exchanged a relieved look.

"Let's get back to work," Anakin said when Sannah had left. He pulled out the papers and started writing symbols down in the place he'd left off. A few more lines and he'd be finished. Then he and Tahiri could begin matching symbols to letters. Once they knew what letter each symbol stood for, they could match them to the words carved in the Palace of the Woolamander. Then, perhaps, they could solve the riddle that enshrouded the globe.

SEVENTEEN

It was hard work. Matching symbols to letters, letters to words. Anakin felt his eyesight beginning to blur. Hours passed and night blanketed the Great Temple. Anakin and Tahiri hadn't slept since they'd returned to the Jedi academy. Anakin had written down the symbols from deep within Sistra. He'd written down Aragon's words. But so far, they weren't having any luck matching symbols to letters. It just didn't make any sense. No matter what they tried, they ended up with gibberish.

"We have to get some sleep," Anakin finally stated.

"Let's try one more time," Tahiri coaxed. "We've got to be doing something wrong." She stared at the lines before her tired eyes. Then tried to insert letters for symbols from left to right, in the pattern of Basic. She even tried to scramble the symbols, replacing first and third letters to see if they made more sense. Nothing. "We're missing something," Tahiri grumbled.

"It's no use," Anakin sighed. "The Massassi were a different race than we are. They used symbols, but that doesn't mean that each stood for one letter like it does in Basic. There's an infinite number of possibilities to translate. It's going to take us weeks, months, maybe years!" he cried in exasperation. Anakin was so caught up in his frustration that he didn't hear the door to his room quietly open.

"I can't sleep," Sannah whispered from the entrance. Anakin's head snapped up and Tahiri whirled around to face the door. "I'm sorry, I didn't mean to startle you." Sannah apologized. "It's just that it's hard to sleep in a new place . . ."

"It's okay, Sannah," Tahiri said gently as she helped Anakin gather the crumpled papers before them. One sheet dropped from her grasp and wafted gently through the air. She watched as it floated—a white bird borne on the winds of chance. The paper landed, faceup, by Sannah's bare feet.

Sannah bent over and picked up the sheet. She moved forward to hand it back to Tahiri. "What is this?" she asked.

"It's just something Aragon told us," Anakin explained as he reached for the paper. Sannah drew it back toward her and curiously studied the scribblings of Basic. Finally, a look of understanding spread across her fine features. Sannah read out loud the words "Peace to all." Then, she giggled.

"What's so funny?" Tahiri asked.

"It's just that I've never seen Basic written so strangely," Sannah replied.

"What do you mean?" Anakin asked intently.

"Well, you've lined the letters up so that Aragon's words run from left to right," Sannah explained. "But on Yavin 8, we spell our words from top to bottom." Sannah crouched by Anakin and took the writing tool from his hand. She turned the sheet over and scribbled one word of Aragon's message down. Then she held the sheet up for Anakin and Tahiri.

P
E
A
C
E

the letters read.

Anakin's ice blue eyes met Tahiri's blazing green ones. The message they exchanged was clear—This is it!

"I'll walk you back to your room and sit with

you until you fall asleep," Tahiri offered Sannah as she took the paper from the girl and casually passed it down to Anakin. Then she took Sannah's hand. "I had trouble sleeping my first night, too," she said kindly. Her words drifted softly through the hallway as she led Sannah back to her room.

Anakin spread his papers back out and began to match symbols to letters. He turned when he heard a soft sound behind him. The Jedi Master Ikrit had appeared on his window ledge. The Master sat silently, watching Anakin with round brown eyes. The young Jedi turned back to his work.

It makes sense, Anakin thought to himself. The Massassi must have learned the pattern that the Melodies wrote in, and assumed that others would write in the same way. That was why they carved their symbols vertically instead of horizontally, left to right. Anakin watched the words of the ancient Massassi from the Palace of the Woolamander come to life beneath his writing tool. By the time Tahiri had returned to his room, he was finished with the translation.

"Did it work?" Tahiri asked breathlessly as she slipped into the stone chair across from her friend.

Anakin didn't answer. Instead he held up the sheet before him and began to read out loud.

"Peace to all. We are the Massassi. Our children have been imprisoned by the evil Jedi Knight Exar Kun. Locked deep within this palace, hidden in the glittering sands of a golden globe, they await. The crystal that holds them prisoner can only be unlocked by children, strong in the Force and dedicated to the battle of good over evil. If you are the ones, enter the globe and lead our children to freedom."

"We're the ones, aren't we?" Tahiri whispered.

"Yes," Anakin replied, his ice blue eyes flashing. "We're the ones." On the window ledge, Ikrit watched. The Force was strong in these two children, he knew. But he knew, too, of the dangers that lay ahead.

PROMISES

Before she joined the academy, Anakin's friend Tahiri lived with a strange and dangerous tribe. She knows nothing of her real parents—or how she came to live with the treacherous Tusken Raiders. Tahiri knew the day would come when she'd learn *everything* about her past . . . and that day has come!

But first, Tahiri must prove she's worthy. And that means she must complete a deadly task that will test her skills as a warrior and a Knight. With Anakin by her side, she will have to use the Force like never before.

If Tahiri succeeds, she will learn how her parents lived— and died. But if she fails, she and Anakin may have to face the *ultimate* price . . .

Turn the page for a special preview
of the next book in the
STAR WARS: JUNIOR JEDI KNIGHTS series:
PROMISES
Coming in April from Boulevard Books!

All thoughts were wiped out of Anakin's mind as a rock-crushing roar filled the air. And this time, it was not the sound of a womp rat. This time it was full of the venom of a different creature. A creature that towered over the Jedi candidates, its massive jaws spread open to reveal a red forked tongue and rows of black teeth that glistened with the greenish ooze of womp rat blood.

"Krayt dragon," Anakin said grimly. The beast was perched on the rocks above them, its head covered with seven black horns, its back ridged with sharp bony nodules and a jagged dorsal spine. The creature's scaly green body was tipped with claws of crimson that matched its reddish eyes—angry eyes, divided by black slit-shaped pupils that stared intently from Anakin to Tahiri and back again.

Anakin slowly stood. "Leave us alone," he commanded in a voice touched with fear and only weakly ringing with the Force. The krayt dragon hissed, but made no move to leave the Jedi candidates. "LEAVE US!" Anakin called out. The dragon screeched, then struck out like lightning, one massive limb batting Anakin into the air. He landed on the rocks, ten meters from where he'd stood. The dragon's claws had ripped through his academy jumpsuit and made five bloody gashes across his rib cage. The sliced skin burned, but Anakin sensed that his wounds weren't deep. "I'm all right, Tahiri," he called. That's when he heard her scream.

Anakin bolted to his feet in time to see the monster moving in on Tahiri. "Stop!" he cried. But the reptile kept advancing toward his friend. "Fight him, Tahiri!" Anakin yelled.

Tahiri rose and tried to strike the dragon with her gaderffii. The creature's crimson eyes flashed as it batted the weapon from Tahiri's grip. Then Tahiri was covered by the dragon's dark shadow. Anakin scrambled across the rocks. He had to save his friend. The dragon turned as he approached. Tahiri was pinned beneath its front legs. The monster's red tongue flicked toward Anakin, as if tasting him. "Let her go!" Anakin growled at the loathsome creature.

The dragon charged Anakin, its eyes flashing.

Anakin's ice blue eyes narrowed as he stared at the advancing monster. There has got to be a way to defeat it, he thought. But a split second later the creature grasped him in its jaw and turned to slither rapidly through the canyon.

Tahiri bolted to her feet. To save Anakin, she had to trail the krayt dragon. She ripped her pack off her back and tore after the beast. It would take all her strength to keep up with the creature, but if she lost sight of it, she wouldn't be able to help her friend.

So, you've decided Anakin is enough for dinner, Tahiri thought grimly as she climbed after the creature. She could feel Anakin's fear as he was carried away. Tahiri raced through the rocks. She only hoped the dragon's lair wasn't far away; the pace was quickly wearing her down. I won't let you down, Anakin, Tahiri thought. There are all kinds of strength—that's what Master Ikrit once told me. And I'm going to find the one that will defeat the dragon.

If the creature sensed her as she followed, it didn't let on. In fact, it seemed to have completely forgotten Tahiri existed. She wondered if the krayt lost its desire to hunt and kill once it found its prey. Tahiri followed the dragon for fifteen minutes as it wound along the rocky canyon. Her breath escaped in ragged streams. She was exhausted, but she wouldn't stop to rest until she had saved Anakin. The monster was widening the distance between them, and Tahiri forced herself to quicken her pace. She hoped that wherever it was heading, there wouldn't be any more dragons. Fighting one was going to be hard enough.

Suddenly, the dragon disappeared. Tahiri's heart sank. Had she fallen so far behind that she'd lost the creature? She stared in every direction—there was no sign of the dragon or Anakin. Her shoulders sagged in defeat and she slowly sat down on a large boulder. Her eyes filled with tears and she angrily shook her head to get rid of the unwanted saltwater.

Out of the corner of one eye, Tahiri noticed a dark hole between two large rocks. She leapt forward. From out of the hole rose an oily smell that burned her eyes and made her gag. She crouched and peered down. She couldn't see anything in the blackness. Tahiri grabbed the rough edges of the hole and dropped in, her body sliding several meters before coming to a stop at the mouth of a rocky tunnel that stretched deep within the mountain. Must be home, she thought wryly. Then she began to creep along the tunnel. Several times she had to step over the remains of what she could only assume were Raiders, judging by the white tattered robes that covered the skeletons. The carcasses of womp rats also lined the tunnel. Tahiri tried to ignore them as she snuck along.

Anakin was crouched in the center of a basically round room, the only light there filtered through the small holes in the ceiling that were exposed to the surface of the mountain. As Tahiri's eyes adjusted, she saw that the lair was also littered with the skeletons of womp rats and some brown-robed remains. The dragon was rustling on the far side of the room. Now that he had Anakin, he didn't seem to be in too much of a rush to eat him. Must be saving him for later, Tahiri thought with deadly calm. All the fear that had initially coursed through her veins had drained away. In its place, she felt the strength of the Force surging through her. There was no way she was going to allow the krayt dragon to hurt her friend.

Anakin sensed Tahiri's presence. He raised his face and peered into the darkness. Slowly he rose to knees, then gained his feet. Tahiri stepped out of the shadows and moved to Anakin's side. The side of his academy jumpsuit was drenched in blood, and Tahiri stifled a cry. Anakin grasped her hand tightly, and for a brief moment their eyes met. The look they exchanged was one of calm and resolve. They would fight this beast together.

The krayt dragon turned and rose on its hind

feet. A thin screech rolled out. Its dinner was being threatened, and that made the reptile angry. Very angry. Slowly the dragon advanced on the Jedi candidates. And in a flash it had snatched Anakin and pinned him beneath its clawed feet.

"My voice didn't work," Anakin groaned to Tahiri. "So we've got to try something else." He stared into the razor teeth that lined the creature's jaws. "And soon, because its breath will kill me if its teeth don't first."

Tahiri stared desperately around the lair for a weapon. Her eyes stopped on a large boulder that jutted out on the far side of the room. Maybe I can distract him, she thought, and then we can try to run. Tahiri closed her eyes and focused on using the Force to pry the boulder loose. Nothing happened.

"Any ideas?" Anakin gasped as the dragon stared down at him with hungry eyes.

"Believe and you succeed," Tahiri murmured to herself as she continued concentrating on the rock. Moments later there was a thunderous crash.